J.R

Burning

Muses

Burning Muses
Copyright © 2016 by J. R. Rogue

RADIANT SKY PUBLISHING GROUP

Publisher's Note: This is a work of fiction. Names, characters, places, and incidents are a product of the author's imagination. Locales and public names are sometimes used for atmospheric purposes. Any resemblance to actual people, living or dead, or to businesses, companies, events, institutions, or locales is completely coincidental.

Editor: Alicia Cook, www.thealiciacook.com
Cover Art: Indie Solutions by Murphy Rae, www.murphyrae.net
Interior Design: JT Formatting

Burning Muses / J. R. Rogue – 1st ed.
ISBN-13: 978-0692666098 | ISBN-10: 0692666095

www.jrrogue.com

Burning Muses

Burn them all!

J. R. *(signature)*

J. R. ROGUE

For the survivors.
You are good.
Never forget this.

A Shitty Sunday, I think

some people are
born fractured.

demons deposited
here among us.

I like to think I was born pure.
that for a while I was like an angel.
(my mother named me after one, after all)

I guess it wasn't in the master plan for me to
stay that way.
this sickness was put inside of me
by familiar hands.

I walk with the pretty people now.
the good.
but I am not.

I am not good.

March 1ˢᵗ

In everyone's life, there are definitive moments that change everything. There are lows you reach that kick off the cycle of changing you for the better. Sometimes you forget those moments; sometimes they stay with you forever. For me, crying in the middle of sex in a Las Vegas hotel room was one that would stay with me until the day I died.

No one wants to be that girl, and no man has anything remotely positive to say after an experience like this. I would never write a scene like this in one of my novellas.

My characters were strong and feisty. Yet here I was, their creator, behaving like the sniveling sidekick; the pathetic best friend with a series of hapless romances attached to her name. To make matters worse, the man on top of me took longer than I liked to notice my tears. When he did, he called me by the ridiculous nickname that he had been using for the past week, making the whole scene seem even direr.

"Aw, Ser-Bear. What's wrong, Babe?" He sounded genuinely concerned. I would give him that; but we were both trashed. 'Babe,' too? I found it hard not to groan.

"Nothing," I mumbled, pushing up on his chest. He disconnected and rolled onto his back, raking his hand across his face. I

1

wondered if he would ask what was wrong again. I told him 'no emotions' between us, and he had kept to that, but my actions now were screaming 'comfort me'. I was not holding up my end of the bargain.

My breakdown had nothing to do with him though. Earlier in the night, I had received a text from my best friend, Kat, from my hometown. "I have news," she announced. Despite my incessant begging, she would not divulge the information, instead saying that she would call me in the morning. I only had one guess that felt right. She was pregnant.

Kat was married for five years now, and I knew she and her husband had been trying for the last two of those. My friend had always been the mothering type; she looked out for me most of my life. She always knew what to do. In high school, our friend Chelsy found herself pregnant our sophomore year and the first person she ran to was Kat. Not her parents, not her boyfriend, not the school counselor. Kat. Kat had an answer for everything, a soothing voice, and a level head.

If she had her way, a baby would have arrived much sooner, but her husband wanted to wait, arguing that his new law firm had to be more financially secure. Despite how this frustrated her, she was supportive of him in every way. If there was any role besides 'mother' that Kat was born to play, it was 'wife.'

I had never been jealous of the life my friend had. I knew it was wonderful and she was lucky, but it was not for me. I had no boyfriends in high school, and dated little in college. Not for lack of attention, I just hated being tied to anyone, and my attention was hard to hold. Plus, it all made for great writing.

I suppose even the most inexperienced woman could write erotica, but I found that real life experience, to some extent, helped immensely, and was terribly fun. Until you are crying during sex, which brings me back to my current predicament.

After reading Kat's text earlier, I felt excitement for her. I bought everyone in the bar a shot, even though she hadn't officially told me. I hooted and hollered; I laughed and told everyone fond stories of Kat. My companions listened to me, drank with me, and eventually grew weary of the stories about some chick from the Midwest they didn't know and could care less about.

Slowly fear and sadness crept inside me. My intoxicated thoughts ran wild. I was in the last half of my 29th year alive and wasted on a Tuesday night. I had never been in a serious relationship, and my current fling with the lead actor of the Vegas show that was running in my hotel, certainly did not count.

I had nothing inside but overwhelming fear when it came to my profession, which had led me to this sad state I was in. This was the proverbial straw on the damn camel's back.

In hindsight, I should have known heading to Vegas for a one-month bender was not the cure to any of my problems. At the time, it seemed like the perfect solution but I was too old for this shit.

I groaned loudly into the room, threw the covers off my legs, and headed to the bathroom. A scalding hot shower always helped somewhat in sobering me up, and I desperately needed to look at this situation with clear eyes.

My companion paid little attention to me as I left the room. From the corner of my eye, I spotted him picking up his phone and quickly beginning to send out a text. *On-to-the-next*, I suppose.

I set the water to the hottest setting and began to undress. I spotted a fresh bruise on my shin and cursed aloud. Why was I so clumsy when I drank? I sank down onto the cool porcelain floor, flipping through images of the night. Every picture in my head made me cringe. Nothing was worth writing about, the same as every night this past month. Same as every night for over a year.

I had flirted endlessly with the hot as hell bartender at Gilley's. He was delicious, if any of my readers read about a man that looked like him they wouldn't be able to control themselves. But I had done this before. I had written about the sexy as fuck bartender that seduces the young innocent protagonist off her feet and introduces her to new and exciting sexual desires. I would not write about the same thing twice. It was writer's suicide.

I had also already written about the sexy singer, so the delicious man in my bed was a waste of my time. Still, I doubted he would complain about the time we had spent together, minus my tiny breakdown earlier.

This was all getting old fast. I was running out of ideas to help the process.

My name is Seraphina Daniels, but the world knows me as 'Lexa Fire.' I have become one of the top ten bestselling erotic writers in the world. My bestselling trilogy, Pinned, was in the productions stages for the film adaptation of the third novel. The first movie was an insane success. I was able to collaborate with the filmmakers on many aspects, and it had been one of the most thrilling experiences of my life, as well as one of the most damning.

My name was everywhere, my work was discussed constantly, and, in turn, sales for all of my books had skyrocketed. All eyes were on me for my next project, and I couldn't write a single fucking word.

I had tried everything I could possibly think of. I had flown to my summer home in Florida, spending night after night upon the beach, day after day living life with the locals. Nothing. Frustrated, I flew to Alaska, always finding the state to be fascinating. I now had an excuse to spend more time there than my book signings would allow. It was beautiful, romantic and splendid. Still, nothing.

Growing more agitated, I flew to the one place I had always wanted to visit, Ireland. That trip was one I would never forget or regret, but no story came from it. I was at the end of my rope.

As a struggling writer, I had always dreamed of visiting beautiful locations upon which to base my stories, always jealous of those successful enough to be able to do so. Now, I was one of them, and I couldn't squeeze one hundred measly words out a day.

I never saw writer's block coming. When the movie rights to the first book had been purchased, the trilogy was still not finished. The first book had been released and the second nearly written. The whole world was obsessed with the story as I wrote the third book. None of this stifled my creative eye. I thrived in it. It thrilled me to know the entire world was in love with the characters I created. The words spilled from my fingertips to the screen. The third book came out timed with the release of the second movie.

The worldwide frenzy and my newfound success was astonishing. I started writing less. I traveled and basked in the glow of what my life had become. When filming began for the third movie, hot on the heels of the second's success, I stayed close to the set. The movies had remained beautifully faithful to my novellas, the female director of the films, becoming one of my closest friends. Months passed by in a blur and I was without a care in the world.

I attended red carpet premieres for the films, the first taking place where I lived, in New York City. I loved the glamour of it all. All day long I would be pampered by hair stylists and makeup artists dolling me up like a star. As a child, I always dreamed of taking the stage in beautiful gowns and singing before audiences of thousands, this dream was quickly forgotten when I realized I couldn't sing worth a damn. This is the closest I would get.

The film's sexy British star, Tristan, was my date for each premiere in the various cities we visited. He was the hottest celebrity in the world. When buzz began over the casting of the first movie, his name was thrown around more than others. My readers knew he embodied every physical characteristic of the lead in my books. I agreed. I fantasized about him starring in the film. I fantasized about other things, too. We were not dating, but walking the red carpet together sent tongues wagging. He was extremely private about his love life and would never bring an actual woman in his life to the red carpet. The speculation over if he was dating the beautiful author of the books was great for tickets sales. We maintained that we were just friends, the truth, but tabloids never believed it. It didn't bother me. If the world wanted to believe I was sleeping with one of the most beautiful men alive, then go for it. It certainly wasn't difficult to gaze at him adoringly for the camera.

The final premiere for film number two was to be just like any other. I was prepared for the onslaught of questions about my next project. I remained coy about the subject. I gave no details, mostly because I had none, but assured everyone I was hard at work. I didn't feel at that time that I had writer's block. I convinced myself I was merely busy, ignoring the fact that I had never gone this long in my life without at least filling my journal. I began writing as a young child to pass the time in our old country home. With no siblings to keep me company, it was one of the many ways I stayed busy. Still, the seed of fear was planted within me and I had yet to admit its presence to myself. I knew I needed a place to hide, but I never expected where I would find it that night.

I was never a particularly brave girl when it came to men without some liquid courage. Small talk was not one of my specialties, and flirting was not second nature to me; but give me a couple Long Island Ice Teas and I suddenly morphed into a much smoother version of myself. Give me too many Long Islands and I become a much sloppier version of that seductress, a mistake I learned the hard way.

I was always told I was too uptight, so a little bit of alcohol went a long way to calm my nerves. That night I got my hand on those drinks, and got in bed with Tristan.

Now, here I was. I stretched my legs out in front of myself in the shower. Letting the hot water beat down, soaking my hair, soaking my fear. I didn't want to think about that night but I couldn't stop myself. Memories from the night of my book's movie premiere came flooding back to me.

I had downed three cranberry vodkas before we sat down to watch the film. I had been on set for most of the filming and viewed bits and pieces during pre-production, but this would be my first time seeing it in its entirety. I was nervous. I was tipsy. I was pissed that I hadn't been writing and had been too busy with this damn movie. I wasn't in the film industry. I was a damn writer. I found my seat next to Tristan just as the room went dark.

I write erotic fiction, yes, but that doesn't mean sex doesn't make me blush. I was sitting in a dark theater next to the man starring on the screen. I was each of my leading characters. I based them off my real life experiences. Seeing the man next to me act out the actions from my past, act out my fantasies, was too much for me that night. I had been through this before with the first film, but at a safer distance away from him. Factor in the alcohol I had already consumed, and I was screwed.

The first sex scene began ten minutes into the film, at this point in the series our lovers were more than acquainted with each other. They began to slowly strip for each other, the scene was too much. I felt my face redden and my breathing pick up slightly. I sensed Tristan noticing my reaction to him on the screen, so I slowed my breathing. I reminded myself that the room was pitch black, and he couldn't see my crimson cheeks.

He couldn't tell that the palm of my hand resting next to his arm was beginning to sweat. I focused on the screen. He was too beautiful. Thirty minutes passed and we came to another sex scene. Jesus.

Okay, yeah, this movie wasn't based on Shakespeare, it was based on my smut book. I really screwed myself with this one. I uncrossed my legs, and then crossed them on the other side. It wasn't helping. Tristan was watching the screen just as I was, but I felt his awareness of me. I felt him inside my head. He must have sensed my frustration. It was tangible. It was one thing to lust after the man voted People Magazine's Sexiest Man Alive in the privacy of your own home, but panting like a rabid fan right next to him was a whole other level of crazy.

Suddenly his arm came up to rest next to mine, his pinkie grazed the side of my hand, and I lost it. I jumped, what I felt, was three feet out of my seat. The person in front of me slightly turned their head to the side, showing me the furrow of their brow. I mumbled an apology, rose to me feet, and motioned for Tristan to move his legs so I could exit the row. The second from the front.

"Everything alright?" He whispered, a smile in his voice.

"Yes, just need to get to the restroom." I brushed past him, practically running to the exit. I found the large bathroom empty. Everyone else was glued to the huge screen. I turned the cold water on, bracing both of my arms on the side of the sink. I watched the water swirl around and quickly spiral down the drain. I focused on the circular motion.

Why was I avoiding writing? My success had been unlike anything I could have imagined. I never set out for it. I wrote my first novella in college. I was casually dating a senior named Adam. He was fun and never spent a moment of his life being serious. Getting a job? Not important. Making it to class? Maybe tomorrow. I knew he wasn't forever, but he helped me let loose. He loved that I enjoyed writing. I would let him read my writing assignments, but never my poetry. I didn't love him, so he could never see that piece of me.

One night he had a crazy idea. We could pretend to be different people. We could role-play and leave all of our inhibitions behind, and then I could write about it. I resisted at first. I couldn't write about our sex lives. "But it won't be us," he argued.

Adam graduated and moved away. We parted on good terms. Our stories had grown stale. I needed a new muse. It did not hurt much to see him go.

My cheeks reddened in the mirror in front of me at the thought of my past, the beginning of all of this madness. If I didn't have tons of expensive makeup expertly painted on my face, I would have splashed the cool water below me on my cheeks. I was going to pull it together, go back to my seat, and watch this movie like a damn adult. The door behind me *whooshed* open, the sound of footsteps closed in on me. Jesus, that was a heavy-footed woman. I looked up into the mirror; Tristan's face stared back at me.

"Son of a bitch!" I yelped. My heart was in my throat. Holy hell. "What are you doing in here?" I croaked.

"I was worried about you."

"This is the women's restroom. Why didn't you just text me? Creeper."

"Good point," he blushed. He was so close to me. I felt his fingertips on my forearm. I stared into his green eyes in the mirror. "You okay to go back out there?"

"Yeah, yeah I guess." I looked back down at my white knuckles gripping porcelain.

"We don't have to. We can stay in here," he offered. His breath was on my neck. My own came in a hiss. We missed the rest of the movie.

March 9th

After my shower, and a long night's unrest, I got myself out of Vegas and flew back to New York. I booked a flight for the next week as well. For Missouri. I would be going home. I couldn't write in the City. I couldn't write anywhere. The last possible option was to go home. I had escaped years ago, and I did not want to go, but I was needed. Kat needed me. I called my friend the day after her vague text. I was wrong, there was no baby on the way, but there was a divorce in the works.

I didn't know what to say. I didn't know how to comfort her. Words were my life and I had none for her. I decided the best thing I could do was go home. To be there for her. To be her best friend again. She could face her future while I confronted my past.

Besides, I couldn't stay in the City. Tristan was there filming. *With her.* The last thing I needed was the paparazzi catching a photo of me with anything but a smile on my face. Oh, how I loved their clever captions. I was no longer the 'girlfriend of a celebrity' and done with the scrutiny that came along with the title.

I spent the next week preparing my apartment to be unoccupied for an undetermined amount of time. I ripped my closet apart, donated half of my wardrobe to Goodwill, and then purchased every cute outfit I could find online, shipping it to my old home in the Midwest. Shopping made me happy. I figured I could hold onto at least one of my vices.

I walked off the jet ramp with my carry-on and made my way through the tiny Springfield airport. The smallness of the building closed in on me immediately. I sauntered towards the exit, spotting my mother right away among the few people waiting for arrivals.

She was wearing a navy knee length dress covered by a lavender cardigan, and cute Oxfords. She always looked like a teacher, even when she wasn't in her classroom. Her shoulder length raven hair framed her beautiful, familiar face. A smile spread ear-to-ear when she caught sight of me. Her prodigal daughter had finally returned.

I choked down my guilt and closed the distance, wrapping my arms tightly around her delicate frame. "I'm so happy to have you back home, Dear," she whispered into my ear.

"Thanks, Mom. Me too." I wasn't sure if I meant those words just yet, but I was happy to see her.

"Let's get out of here." She linked her arm with mine and we set off. March's crisp Missouri morning air whipped my long jet hair around as we made it outside. I pulled my sleeves down from my elbows, one by one, covering the ink on my arms.

"I've made up the spare room for you. It looks really nice. Redecorated it just last month."

"Mom. I told you. I want to stay at Grandma and Grandpa's

old house. I'll need plenty of quiet time to write. This isn't a vacation." The only one in the City who knew about my past was my therapist.

I was an avoider. She reminded me of this, every session. She did not treat me with 'kid's gloves'. I distracted myself with men and liquor. With casual phone conversations with my mother, always avoiding the truth of my dark heart. During my last therapy session, she reminded me of my strengths. I felt like she was talking about a stranger when she listed them. She believed going home would be helpful. I wasn't sure if I agreed, but I was here, none the less.

"Well I was just thinking it'd be nice to spend time together and have you in the same house," my mother said, pulling me from my thoughts.

"We will spend time together. Don't worry. This isn't going to be a short trip..."

"Be sure to make time for other things while you're here too," she baited. "Maybe you can find a nice guy to settle down with."

I tripped over the sidewalk curb and aimed an annoyed set of eyes at her. "I seriously doubt there is anyone in Missouri I would like to date. I just got out of a relationship. And mom, this isn't the fifties. There is no certain age I need to be married by. That's the way small little towns like this are, but not where I live. Too many people settle here. They settle for about anyone who will have them. It's sad. I'm not doing that crap. There is a whole big world out there with millions of people from which to choose. I don't need anyone to take care of me so I'll get married when I want." My voice was a little loud, and a lot defensive.

"You know I don't believe women need to marry young. I didn't. I'm just saying though, I'd like to see you as happy as I am."

"No men right now." It was a reminder for her as well as myself.

"Well anyways. I hope you end up staying through summer. I miss you so much. Everyone does."

"How are you feeling about this school year coming to an end? No more teaching." I still couldn't believe she was retiring. I had always assumed she would continue until she was white haired and arch-backed.

"I'm ready. I'm emotional, too. It's hard." She waived her hand in the air absently. I knew the sign. She was more upset than she let on. "Now why did I see only one small suitcase in your hand? Are you going to wear the same outfit over and over?"

"Look who you're talking to. C'mon, Mom, seriously. No, I plan to go shopping as soon as possible. It was easier than lugging a bunch of my stuff down here. I'll hit the mall as soon as I get settled. And I did some online shopping before I left. A bunch of boxes should be arriving soon. You know me and retail therapy."

"Oh yes, Dear, you've never grown out of that one. And about Grandma and Grandpa's, I need to tell you something. We have someone living there."

"Who?" I stopped at the back of my mother's car.

"Andrew's friend, Chace. They have been attached at the hip ever since they were kids. Remember the one I told you lived with us his senior year? You've heard me talk about him. The one who was living with us for quite a while." I stared back with a blank face, not knowing who she meant. "Anyways, I told you the house needed work. And the landscaping is downright scary. He is taking care of all of that, on top of his job and schoolwork. I promise you will have quiet time out there. He is going to school to be a teacher."

"Oh, you must love him then," I laughed, making my way for the passenger door.

"He is a fine young man," my mother replied as she got behind the wheel. "I wish Andrew would take after him more."

My stepbrother, Andrew, was not exactly on the 'right track' in life. After flunking out of his freshman year of college at USC, he moved back home, quickly getting a job at one of the local furniture factories. Six months later, he was fired from that job and spent the next four months unemployed. From what I heard, he was now doing construction for a father of one of his high school friends. Growing up didn't seem to be a priority of his. I loved him dearly though. Despite our seven-year age difference, I still considered him as close as any blood relative I had.

"That would be nice," I replied, not wanting to dwell too much on the subject. He would figure it out. I hoped.

"If you need Chace to help you with anything around the house I know he would be more than happy to. He is just a good kid. He went to Lowe's with me last week and helped pick out all the flowers for the front of the house. I believe they are actually delivering all of those today."

"I bet Paul is glad to get out of that duty." My stepfather never got in the way of my mother's projects but he tried to get out of helping at all costs.

"Oh, yes. You know he never much cared for decorating or any of the house stuff."

"Well, I'm already loving seeing all of this wide open space. And the woods. I can't wait to see our woods again."

"Be careful out there, Hun."

"Mom, I'm almost 30. You let me run all over that property when I was a kid! And I've been living in a city for years now. I think if anything was to happen to me it would have happened there."

"True."

"It's been too long though honestly. I might get a bit freaked out. I think I've watched too many horror movies."

"You and those dang movies. I'll never understand why you like to scare the dickens out of yourself."

"Fear is one of the purest emotions. I love it. Maybe if you had let me watch them more growing up, I would have grown out of them. Now I have to make up for lost time." She laughed loudly in response. I missed my mother's laugh. The long drive flew by.

After an hour and a half drive on the interstate we found the exit to my hometown. It was smaller, and dirtier, than I remembered. We passed through the lone stoplight and out of town. My stomach started to ache as we passed the city limit sign.

My grandparent's home was located just five miles from town, but it felt like another world. When we turned to make our way down the mile long driveway I felt my heart twitch. Maybe this was a bad idea.

The three-story farmhouse was located on 80 acres, only 12 of those free of woods. On that land, you could find two creeks, three ponds, and hundreds of places for a child to run wild. Without a brother or sister to play with, I was often left to my own devices, with nothing more than my imagination to keep me entertained. Luckily that was something I had in abundance.

My mother always encouraged regular reading, but like any young kid, I would get restless and crave the outdoors. I would spend my weekends outside all day long, only briefly coming inside to eat my meals, shoveling down my food just to rush back into my own world. I was warned to always stay close enough so that someone could yell for me to come inside, although this was a rule I didn't always adhere to.

I always carried a notebook with me, something else my mother encouraged. I would write plays and act them out for the squirrels jumping from tree to tree. I fancied that they enjoyed my shows from their screaming, although now I know they only wanted me to get out from under their tree.

I would climb trees and write stories about a group of survivors living in the treetops in a world overrun by zombies (the inspiration for this came from secretly watching Night of the Living Dead.)

In the winter, I would cross the frozen ponds (something I was later forbidden to do) and write about a woman joining hundreds of men braving the elements in the time of the Alaskan gold rush. As a child, I couldn't travel the world for my stories, but I could bring any place I dreamed to life on my grandparent's land. When I was young, my journals and stories were always shared with my grandparents and my mother. Well, almost all of my journals.

On Friday nights the four of us would gather in the living room after dinner to read. Although we owned a television, it was not our primary source of entertainment. I would read aloud a new story most weeks. I was never shy about sharing my words with a room full of teachers. My mom was my thesaurus, often taking notes and suggesting new words for me to use when I was done, never pressuring me to change anything.

All of those pleasant memories came back to me as the large house came into view, pushing down my dread, momentarily.

In the beginning of my career as a writer, my mother found it very hard to let me buy her anything. She was stubborn as an ox. She reminded me constantly that I was the kid and she was the parent. If there was anything she was ever passionate about, besides teaching, it was the house we grew up in. Interior decorating was a talent of hers. I can recall countless Saturdays begrudgingly accompanying her to antique malls and swap meets. Our three-story home was once an old farmhouse and she wanted to keep that look.

For many years, she fantasized about turning it into a Bed and Breakfast, eventually deciding something inside the city limits would be more suited for the project. After over a year of pleading and explaining to her that it would be an investment for me, she let me buy our old home from her, which freed her up to buy another home perfect for the B&B. I wanted to own that house. I wanted to be in control of its future. I wanted to have the power to burn it to the ground if I saw fit. My mother finally gave in so that her parent's home would stay in the family forever, something she had always hoped.

I could see now that it needed some work. Time and weather had left their marks. Leaving an older house uninhabited would change it. For years, I fantasized about having it leveled with a bulldozer, but the happy memories I had there, swayed me.

There was a black jeep with a small trailer parked by the side of the house. Large plastic bags and plants were loaded on it. My new roommate, Chace, stood on the trailer with a bag over his shoulder. He turned at the sound of gravel crunching. He threw the bag down and stepped off, walking towards our idle vehicle. There was something strange in his step. "What's he like?" I tossed the question to my mother as I opened the door.

She turned to me and smiled, opening hers. "They don't make them any better."

Chace was upon us as soon as I made my way to the front of the car. He was dressed in a grey shirt, old jeans, and worn black converse. He was covered in soil and sweat. His smile was small as he glanced at me, wider when it rested on my mother. A large husky trailed behind him.

"Good morning, ladies," he greeted. His voice did not fit his appearance. He was tall, over six feet, with broad shoulders and solid arms. He had a gym membership no doubt. His voice was soft, not feminine, but comforting. "How was your flight? I'm Chace." He stepped forward and offered his hand after wiping it on his jeans.

I stepped closer and took it. It was large, and a bit warm and sweaty still. "Sera. The daughter. Hi. Flight was good. Thanks."

"You look like you have had a productive morning already," my mom cut in. "Did you charge that to the Lowe's account I set up?"

"Yep. I figured I should pick up some of the stuff I needed before class today. Do you have any idea what you want me to do here?" He began walking towards the front of the house, we followed.

"No, I trust whatever you do. Or you can ask Sera here. It's technically her house."

Thanks mom. I owned the house but I knew nothing about landscaping and had no desire to learn anything about flowers, shrubbery, or saplings. It wasn't something a New Yorker had to worry oneself with.

"I don't care what you do, either. I guess just make it look pretty." Just no fucking tulips. He smiled lightly at me in response, and focused on my mother.

"Okay, that's settled then," my mother decided. "Sera, I'm going to head home. Let's get together this weekend? Sunday lunch out at the house with us?"

"Yes, that works. I'll get my suitcase."

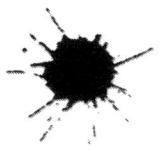

I walked wide-eyed into my mother's old room and was instantly comforted by how little had changed inside this particular space. Her king sized bed still sat against the far wall, one large window to the right of it, the glass door leading to the balcony on the left. I had long been envious of the balcony. On warm summer nights, my mother would let me put our small pop-up tent out there to sleep. She felt it was safer than having me out in the yard alone.

I remember sitting cross-legged on the deck with a candle in front of me, telling ghost stories to her. Many nights I would end up inside sleeping next to her after having spooked myself. She always encouraged me to write these tales down, bragging that I could be the next Stephen King, but it never appealed to me. I was more interested in writing fantasy and poetry.

I wheeled my carry-on next to the bathroom door and started for the bed. I was exhausted. Traveling absolutely killed me. I could easily stay in bed the rest of the day, and it wasn't even noon yet. I was getting old.

I pulled out my phone and shot Kat a text message, confirming lunch was at 1 o'clock. She was planning to come out to get me, since I did not have a vehicle yet. I had ordered one badass car, though. One thing I would enjoy about being in the Ozarks would be the beautiful long drives.

My phone dinged just as I heard a knock on the door to my new room. I rolled over to see Chace standing in my open door. His frame dominated the small opening. "I'm going through town on my way to class. Do you need a ride anywhere? I noticed you don't have a car. I'd hate for you to be stranded the rest of the day. There isn't much to eat in the fridge; I normally get groceries on Fridays."

"Actually, yes, that would be great. I was planning to see my friend today. This way she doesn't have to drive all the way out here on her lunch. Thanks."

"No problem. I'm leaving in about ten."

"Okay, I'll be down." He turned and I made my way over to my suitcase and threw it on its side, looking for a hair tie. I noticed earlier that the top was off his jeep. My long hair would be a complete rat's nest by the time we made it into town. After finding one and securing my locks I grabbed my phone, again, to text Kat.

Me: You don't have to come out and get me now. The guy that lives in the house is going to run me into town in a bit. I'll just hang out in your store until lunch if that works.
Kat: That's great! I can't wait to see you :)

Having to rely on other people to leave the property was strange. I hadn't owned a car since high school, having no need for one in New York. Before leaving Las Vegas, I started calling dealerships in Missouri. I had a specific car I wanted, and I needed every option on it. Tomorrow I would be picking up my new Mustang. It was not a vehicle that would be useful for the winters here, but it was already March and I did not intend to stay that long. A couple of months should be enough to get my mind, and Kat, back on track.

I walked to the bathroom, stepping over the tile onto the rug, and took a seat at the large ornate vanity. I always loved watching my mother sit on the plush velvet seat under the warm glow of the three bulbs hanging over the large mirror. I would gaze at her as she put on her makeup. "Leaning over a sink to put your makeup on is no way to live, Dear," she would say. "Just like your writing, it's an art. It shouldn't be rushed. You want to take a seat and stay awhile."

She purchased a small vanity for me at a yard sale a few years later. It wasn't as grand as hers, but it got the job done. I didn't have space for it in my dorm room, but I had it sent to my first apartment. Sure, I could have purchased a new one, but it wouldn't have been the same. It was so strange to be back in this house.

March 9th

After a quick refresher on my makeup and a change of my shirt, I stood outside of Chace's jeep and waited for him to leave the house. He soon came bounding down the front stairs to me, hair glistening wet. "Here ya go." He held out a set of keys to me. "Your mom had me make a copy of mine for you. The front one sticks a bit."

"Yeah, I remember." I took them quickly from his outstretched hand.

"Has it changed much?" He opened his door and hopped in, I did as well.

"Yes and no. I haven't been back since Christmas break, senior year of college. You have this picture in your mind of a place, and when you see it again it's the same, yet not. I don't know if that makes sense."

I looked around at the trees. Buds of green were beginning to grow and the sky was clear. I focused on my old tree house in the distance. You could see it this time of year. The skeleton frame of it was watching me. My grandfather had built it for me. I stared back at the house, the one he had also built, then back at my hands resting in my lap. I clenched them and then released.

"I think it does," Chace replied, breaking my trance.

We headed down the road in silence for a few minutes. I tried to drum up something to discuss. Small talk was never my specialty. Finally, I thought of something.

"So, my mom says the weather has been bad lately." Great, Sera. You brought up the weather. How lame can you be? He smiled despite my boring topic. It was a nice smile.

"Yeah, it's been way too cold. I know we don't live in the south or anything, but it felt like Michigan or something. I'm glad it's finally warming up."

"Have you been to Michigan?"

"No." The corner of his mouth turned up. "When I think of the weather we have had I just immediately think 'Michigan.' Don't ask why."

"Well, I'm glad you're there at the house to help with everything. Having a house just sit without anyone to care for it is no good."

"It works out well. And there is a lot that needs to be done. So, New York City, huh? Why are you here now? If I can ask."

"Well, I need you to drop me on Commercial Street when we get to town at my best friend's store. She is going through a divorce so I wanted to come home to see her. That's mostly why I am here." And to escape a crap breakup, and to convince myself again that I am a writer, and to face that secret-swallowing house. Some things were too much to share with a stranger.

"Your mom said you were moving home. It's just a visit?"

"It's an extended visit. I don't know when I will be going back."

"I see."

"So what are you going to school for?" I already knew the answer.

"I'm going to be a teacher."

"Ah, okay. It makes sense now then." I faked it some more.

"What does?" His eyebrow raised in my direction.

"Why my mom is helping you. She's a teacher; you're going to be a teacher. She really wanted me to be one as well."

"But now you're a writer. That's amazing. I can't imagine the patience it would take to write a book. Some days I feel like I can barely write a song."

"You're a song writer?" Please say no. Hello, kryptonite. Good thing he is young.

"I have a friend in a band and I help out with lyrics from time to time." He laughed suddenly. "I mean, your brother. Your brother is the friend in the band."

"Wait, he is in a band? I didn't know that. I knew he wanted to start one. Damn, I'm a shit sister." I needed to get my head out of my ass. How did I not know this? "But songwriting, that's a form of writing I have never been able to master. I wrote poetry a lot as a teen. Which I am sure if I saw now, I would burn. And I've never had one of my novels published."

"What? But your mom said..."

"Well, I've had a ton of novellas published. The three novels I wrote in college are stored away. Never seen by the public eye."

"Oh."

"So why aren't you in my brother's band?"

"I don't sing and it's not really my 'thing' to be on stage. I mean, once when one of the guitarists was sick I filled in, but that's about it."

"*Can* you sing?" He needed to say no. Singers were like candy to me. His smile alone was making me blush already.

"Nah." He laughed. I couldn't decipher if he was telling the truth or just being modest. I decided he was a horrendous singer. Choosing that option was the best idea. Lusting after the young man who lived with me was no way to start out this getaway. We fell into a silence as we entered town and approached Commercial. I pointed him in the direction of Kat's shop; an empty spot was located just outside her door.

"Thanks for the ride. I guess I'll see you at the house later."

"Okay. Let me get your number that way we can get a hold of each other if we need to."

I reached down and grabbed his iPhone from the center console, quickly inputting my information. "There ya go." I smiled as I hopped out of the jeep.

A wooden bench sat outside the entrance to Kat's shop. A young girl sat there. She was staring at me. I looked into her eyes and her gaze quickly darted to the phone in her hand. She stood and walked past me, never averting her eyes from the phone, furiously typing. I caught her in the reflection of the glass door as she stepped off the curb and reached for Chace's passenger side door.

Kat was part owner of a small boutique in the town's old square. She shared ownership with Alicia, a classmate who graduated a few years after us. I couldn't put a face to the familiar name when Kat told me years ago about the partnership.

Kat was the buyer for everything they sold, while Alicia took care of the financials and the staff, which consisted of one full time employee and three part-time. They sold a variety of items, ranging from jewelry down to candles and home decor. A small bell above me jingled as I entered. The two glass windows on my sides had many live plants in them. The smell of butterscotch tickled my nose.

"Welcome to Fiddlesticks," someone said from the register.

"Hi, I'm looking for Kat?" I said, picking up a cute vase on a table.

"Just a moment. I'll go get her from the back." The employee retreated to hunt down my friend and I picked a wall to explore. I was instantly proud of my pal. The atmosphere was inviting, the merchandising on par with anything I had seen in New York. Sparkling lights hung all over the ceilings, twisted with what looked like sheer curtain panels. Rustic bookcases were angled across the space, holding an eclectic array of products. The walls were lined with dresses and blouses. It was quite adorable. I heard the sound of my ginger friend's voice behind me.

"There she is. In the flesh. The brilliant writer. The red carpet fashionista!"

I spun on my heel and held up my hand to silence her. "You're going to make me blush, knock it off." Her red hair was much longer than it had been the last time she visited, and she was noticeably thinner.

She had only told me a week ago of her surprise that her husband wanted a divorce. Was this gauntness the result of barely eating the past week? Or had things been rough longer than she let on between them? I reached out to her for a hug. She felt tiny in my arms. I was six inches shorter than her, but I would guess that our weight was close now, and I was *New York-skinny*. She squeezed me tightly.

"You have no idea how glad I am you're here. I need you."

"You have me." I rubbed her back gently "I'm not leaving unless I have your approval." I released her and gave her my serious eye squint. I meant it.

"Then, never. How is never?" She mock pouted.

"Now you're just getting greedy. Other people love me too, you know."

She playfully swatted at my arm and grinned. "Oh, I know. I've read every magazine article about you. Everyone loves you! You go to Hollywood parties and date movie stars," she teased.

"*One* movie star." I was never going to escape this.

"*The* movie star. Shit. I'm sorry. Every time someone asks me about my ex-husband I want to cry all over again, and here I am bringing your ex up too. Shit."

"It's no big deal. It wasn't a bad break up." That was the truth, too. There was no yelling, no crying, and no begging on either end; which further justified my reason for ending it. There was nothing deep there. He had been the first man in years I had fell for without turning it into a story. Which was a shame, considering how mind blowing the sex was.

I still had not found *him*. The man to make me write something meaningful for once. The man to touch my skin without bringing dirt forth. I changed the subject, knowing it would come up again that evening. "So, where are we doing dinner later tonight?"

I spent the rest of the afternoon helping my friend around her store. She caught me up on small town gossip while I helped her move boxes around in the back room and checked-in a new shipment that FedEx dropped off after lunch. The hours passed quickly.

For dinner, Kat had chosen her favorite restaurant, Fire, one town over. I didn't expect anything else and made a point to grab a decent amount of cash for a tip. We hadn't seen each other in years. This wasn't going to be cheap.

The atmosphere at Fire was one of its biggest draws; it made me forget I was in the middle of the Midwest. There were two levels, each one suited to different needs and we had a reservation on the underground level.

Upstairs had a more casual feel, weekdays I imagined it was littered with 9-5ers grabbing cocktails before heading home, the lower level was a perfect spot for an intimate date or, in our case, a get together with your closest friend. The waiter led us to a table in a back corner. I wasted no time asking him to bring out a bottle of my favorite wine. He bowed and left, saying he would come back for our food order.

"I can't believe I'm back here," I stated, grabbing my napkin and arranging it in my lap.

"I know," Kat agreed. "I never thought you would come back again."

"I know. I'm sorry I haven't visited." Kat and I were inseparable all through high school and college. When we earned our degrees, I opted to stay in the City. We vowed to stay in touch and for her to come visit after she returned to the Ozarks. Soon, she got married and my first novella hit it big, which made it harder and harder to stay close.

"I'm sure it's difficult to find time. With the movies and the writing. And, Tristan. I still can't believe it."

"You and me both."

"Are you over him?"

"More or less. He's just a normal guy when it comes down to it."

"Um, have you looked around?" She motioned around the room. "*These* are normal guys. Tristan Kane is not. Are the magazines right about him? About what happened? I wanted to text you and ask but it felt tacky. Then I thought I'd call, but, I don't know. I'm sorry. I should have asked. I was just so wrapped up in what was going on in my marriage."

"It's not like you're the only one who has done that. I was so caught up in the thing I had with him I needed to step away. And yes, it was true. He cheated. But it was just a year of my life. It's nothing in comparison to what you have going on. I just needed to get away from it all. I stopped writing. I haven't written anything in over a year."

"Oh, wow."

"Yeah, my publisher is freaking out. I should have had something new out a long ass time ago. They wanted it hot on the heels of the success of the trilogy and movies. I've always had ideas bursting out of me."

In high school I couldn't stop writing poems about that idiot Rex. In college it was my damn reckless side that started this whole career of writing about sex.

"I think I'm tapped out," I said.

"You're telling me you were with Tristan for a year and it didn't inspire you at all?"

"I could never write about us. Do you know what kind of shit storm that would have caused? I can see the headlines now 'JILTED AUTHOR EXPLOITS RELATIONSHIP WITH MOVIE STAR.'"

"True."

"Enough of that crap. Tell me how you're doing." Earlier at Kat's shop, I brought up her husband a couple times to no avail. She said she didn't want to cry at work so I left it alone and busied myself attending to my social media duties while she worked on paper work. Now that we were away from the shop, I wanted to test the waters again.

My friend's eyes immediately welled just as the server came back. She whipped her menu in front of her face. I took my time ordering, asking questions about the chicken. By the time I had made my selection, Kat appeared fine. As soon as our server was gone, her eyes filled again. She told me everything. Everything she had kept from me, so I wouldn't think her marriage was flawed.

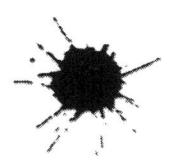

As I suspected dinner lasted many hours, and our tab was large. On the way home, Kat and I sat in silence, content in the low sounds of the radio, lost in our own thoughts. After hearing the whole story, I decided she was better off without her husband, but I kept my opinion to myself for the time being. She needed to process it all, without me chiming in with my opinion. It would be there when she asked.

She left me with a promise to have lunch again the next day. By then I would have my car and would be able to pick her up. I fumbled in my purse for my new key. The wine was making my head fuzzy. I found the key and opened the door, stepping into the house. I slipped my shoes off and quietly made my way up the wooden staircase.

I didn't want to wake Chace. Maybe he was up with little miss nose-in-her-phone. I successfully made it to my room without any loud crashes and fell face first onto the large white comforter for the second time that day. I had been lying there for a couple minutes when I heard the door below me shut.

The living room was right below my bedroom. It had a direct door to the outside that led to the large wrap around porch. I crawled to the side of my bed and reached for my discarded purse, digging for my iPhone to charge it. I heard a guitar and paused. I pulled myself slowly from the bed and tiptoed over to my balcony door. Could I open it without making a sound? This damn house creaked like no other. I chanced it, slowly turning the knob and inching the heavy door open. No sound on my end. Thank you, Jesus.

I sat down in the doorway, listening to his guitar, leaning my back against the doorframe, propping my feet up on the other end. The music stopped and I held my breath. If he caught me listening, I would have to avoid him for at least a week. We had barely spoken, and becoming that creepy lady living in the house with him was not my goal.

I wondered if this was the time of night he always played, or if he chose now because he assumed I would be fast sleep. If an audience bothered him, I would be a horrible housemate. He would quickly notice that I was a night owl, preferring to write, or attempt to write, into the twilight hours.

The setting felt ideal. It was peaceful out here. I had forgotten the sound of the cicadas at night, the soft howl of a coyote in the distance, soon accompanied by his brethren. It was everything I hoped for. If I couldn't find my writing again out here I should just hand in my laptop and give up. The guitar picked up again and I exhaled.

The melody was soft and soothing. I knew I shouldn't be sitting here, very obviously invading his privacy. He seemed shy, and already told me he had only taken the stage to fill in for another.

I made myself as silent as the light wind I felt on my bare arm, better to be safe than sorry. He played for about a half hour, and not a single word escaped his lips. I had hoped to see if he was serious about not being able to sing.

Musicians fascinated me. My friend Andi, a fellow writer, and I would often go to jazz bars and listen to the amazing music. It wasn't my favorite type of music but I grew to appreciate it. We would gather a few of our mutual girlfriends once a month and have "Gatsby Nights." We'd dress up in glitzy jewelry, flapper dresses, and set our hair in beautiful waves. I attracted the attention of a sexy baritone player on one of our fun nights out, soon he and I were having our own fun nights, and in turn, I wrote a very sexy Novella.

The porch below grew silent. Minutes stretched out. Had he snuck inside? I slowly moved from my spot, legs numb from being in one position too long. I brought my legs around into the house and flattened my stomach across the doorway, bringing my eye to a small crack between the boards.

I couldn't see much, but I saw Chace sitting in one of the wicker chairs below. His guitar was still in his lap, his left hand held a pen over a notebook. He had been writing in his silence. Yet he never sang a word aloud. Fascinating.

I didn't personally know any songwriters. I wondered how many others practiced this way. I had many writer friends and there seemed to be a million ways we went about our craft. Some mapped out their entire story, chapter by chapter, breaking everything down. Some simply wrote out their synopsis and went from there. I started with my first sex scene. If I couldn't write my characters getting it on from the beginning, then there was no story to tell. I started there, with no names for my duo, just got right down to the nitty gritty.

Considering the inspiration for my stories, I was not surprised by my method. The story was secondary to the sex. My readers didn't buy my books because they were looking for a Nicholas Sparks' romance. They were looking for something to light their fire, something to perhaps put a little pep back into their relationships.

Chace lifted his guitar from his lap and set in on the deck, then reached for his phone. He propped his feet up on the small ottoman in front of him and began tapping out a text. When he was finished, he reached for his guitar again and began playing. Inside, I heard my phone ding. I slid up to my knees and walked on them over to my bed where my iPhone laid. It was from Chace.

Chace: Did I wake you?

Shit. How could I be so idiotic? Of course he was going to hear me up here like a big creeper. Okay. Act cool.

Me: With the 'did I wake you?' text?
Chace: Haha, no with the guitar.
Me: I was already awake. You didn't hear me come in about five min ago?
Chace: No. Good. Sorry. It's the best time for me to write.
Me: Ditto
Chace: Am I interrupting your writing then?
Me: Not tonight. I'm in a slump.
Chace: The block huh? Pretty bad?
Me: So bad I moved to Missouri.
Chace: Damn. Yes. That is bad.

Me: I'm doomed.

Chace: No, you'll get it back. How long has it been?

It was painful to say. Especially to another writer. Any kind of writer. I could see the pity on their faces. I was thankful he was a full floor below me.

Me: I haven't been able to write in over a year...

Chace: Oh...

Me: Yeah. Doomed. I hope I won't interrupt your playing when I throw myself from this balcony.

Chace: Dramatic, much? All that will get you is a broken arm and wounded pride.

Me: Well, I already have one of those. Hey. You stopped playing.

Chace: I am a man of many talents, Sera. But texting and playing the guitar simultaneously is one I have yet to master.

Me: Smart ass.

Chace: :)

Me: Ok, I won't text you anymore. Play on.

Chace: As you wish.

Did this kid just quote The Princess Bride to me? His personality was different in text. More confident. Although that was common in many people. I listened to him play for ten more minutes before deciding to head to bed. Sleep took me swiftly.

March 10th

The next morning, a call from the car dealership woke me up around eight. A salesman was on his way to drop off my new Mustang. I thanked him and rolled over, burying my face into the pillow. There was a warm breeze flowing through my open window. Perhaps spring was finally arriving. I sighed and whipped the comforter off my body and padded my way to the bathroom. I rushed through brushing my teeth and applied moisturizer to my face. I threw on a pair of black leggings, an oversized t-shirt, and slipped on my white converse.

I half-jogged down the stairs to go outside but the scent of maple syrup stopped me in my tracks. Chace must have made something for breakfast. I sauntered over to the counter, my eyes catching a note on the island that read '*Your food is in the microwave.*' He had used a typewriter to write it. I liked that. I opened the door to find pancakes, sausage, and eggs on a plate. My stomach grumbled. I ate quickly and then went outside.

Chace, and a kid I didn't recognize, were trading free throws back and forth at my old basketball hoop above the door of the detached garage. Chace sank the ball from the edge of the pavement and smiled at me.

"Morning," he greeted.

"Morning." I bent my elbow slightly and waved. "Thanks for the breakfast."

"No problem." He shrugged, and then began dribbling the ball around the driveway. The kid turned to me and smiled. I gave another half wave. I never knew what to say to kids.

"Hi," he beamed.

"Are you, uh, Chace's brother?" I really didn't know much about my new roommate.

"No."

"Oh." I looked up to see Chace's shy grin again.

"Are you Chace's girlfriend?" The child returned.

"No. I think I'm a little old for that." I instantly regretted what I said. I glanced at Chace with my red face and was greeted with his grin again, along with a questioning eyebrow.

"Well, you don't look old," the child responded.

"Thanks. The gray hairs I've been finding would argue with you on that." I reached up and ran my fingers through my long locks. I needed to look through them again to see if another evil gray bastard had emerged.

"Do you live here?" This kid would be great at twenty questions.

"Yes."

"But you're not Chace's girlfriend?"

"No. I'm his roommate."

"Oh. Is that your car in the garage?"

"No. That's my mother's old mustang." And soon I would have my own.

"I like it."

"Me too," I agreed.

"Are you going to play basketball with us?"

"No, I don't really play sports. At all. I'm very bad at them."

"Okay cool." He turned to Chace. "Can I use the restroom?"

"You know you don't have to ask." Chace sunk the ball again.

"'Kay." With that, he took off towards the house. I took a seat on the bench next to the garage. Chace walked towards me with the ball under his arm.

"Sooo. That's Aiden," Chace explained.

"Cute kid."

"Yeah. I used to tutor him. He doesn't get much attention at home."

"That stinks." Growing up, I always received attention from my family. Whether I wanted it or not.

"Yeah. So I try to get him out of his house as much as I can."

"That's really nice of you."

"I try. Did we wake you?"

"No I just got a phone call. Dealership is on their way to drop off my new car. Otherwise I guess I wouldn't be up. I don't keep normal hours."

"True. So, do you have big plans for your first weekend back in the Ozarks?"

"Ah, probably go over to my friend Kat's and help her with her new place. I need to keep her as busy as I can."

"You should come out to Senor's tonight. I'm working."

"That's the new Mexican restaurant right? I think Kat might have mentioned it."

"Yeah. They have a deal on fajitas on Fridays. But come to the bar's side. I work over there."

"I'll run it by her."

When Friday night rolled around, I was able to convince Kat to leave her apartment for dinner and a movie. So far, she had been ordering in pizza and Chinese food. How she was managing to stay so thin living off such unhealthy food was beyond me.

She ducked out of work a bit early so we could catch the 4:30 show of the new Hugh Jackman movie. Kat went to see every film he was in, so he had definitely helped in getting her out of the house. After the flick, we headed to Senor's. Although she protested, I ordered two appetizers as soon as we sat down. I spotted Chace behind the small bar.

"That's way too much food. I won't be able to eat my meal," Kat groaned.

"Tough. You need to fatten up a bit, Missy." I crossed my arms, aiming a motherly look at her. For once, I was the one taking care of her.

"I just never feel like eating."

I had been there for many friends during bad breakups. I had seen them go weeks without many meals. I had never been that upset by a split. Not even Tristan. "I know. But I'm afraid a strong gust of wind is going to blow you away."

"Drama Queen." She waved her napkin at me and laughed. "So, how are things out at the house? You like it there?"

"Yeah it's nice so far, hard to tell this early. I wish I didn't have my iPhone or iPad. There's no internet there now and I could just be off the grid."

"What? No, you're in love with technology. I could live out there and do that. Not you." She pointed to my huge iPhone that was face up on the table beside me.

"Just because I know how to use Twitter and you don't, doesn't mean I am in love with technology." It was a lie.

"How's the roommate?"

I glanced over at Chace behind the bar. "He is a really nice kid."

"Do you know much about him?"

"Just some of what Mom has told me over the years, and a little bit he mentioned when he dropped me at your shop Monday. He is going to school to be a teacher. Um, he graduated with Andrew. I guess they were close in high school. He writes music for Andrew's band, which I did not know existed because I am a shitty sister."

"What does he look like?"

I bit my lip and motioned with my thumb lowly for her to look behind me. "He looks like the bartender."

"Oh, *reallllly?*" She peeked around my shoulder. "That guy is hot."

"Yeah, that's him."

"Oh! He *is* the bartender! He's...pretty."

"Nope," I shook my head. "I don't see it."

"Are you kidding me?"

"I'm not blind, Kat. I'm choosing to ignore the fact that he is appealing." I had done the bartender story arc before. It wasn't going to light any new fires under my ass. I wanted to write something fresh. I would never repeat an idea from within my own work. "Mr. Bartender is young. He has many years of breaking hearts ahead of him."

"How old is he?"

"He is twenty-two. Fun Fact: I'm pretty sure he has a girl-friend."

"Yeah, probably." She shrugged, taking my cue. "How's your mom?"

"Good. I am supposed to go over for lunch on Sunday. It'll be nice to see my brother. It feels like forever. I haven't seen him in two years. He's always too busy to fly out with Mom and his father. Which is strange considering how hard it is for him to keep a job apparently."

"I haven't seen him since he was a little kid! I can't believe he is an adult now."

"Well, you and I are old as dirt now, so it shouldn't be a surprise."

"True. But isn't 30 the new 20 these days?"

I looked over at the loud table next to us, filled with kids around that age. "I wish." The waitress returned, taking our entree order. Just as she was walking off, my phone dinged and I was staring at Chace's name on the screen. I pulled his text up.

Chace: Come up to the bar. I'll buy you two a drink.

"Do you want a margarita?" I asked my friend.

"Sure. Frozen, strawberry."

"Okay." I pushed off the table and turned for the bar. I found an opening next to an empty stool on the end. I wedged myself between it and the wall. The man on the stool next to it immediately turned to me and smiled. I smiled back. Chace was further down the bar taking an order. I saw his eyes quickly dart my direction then back to his customer.

"Well, just who are you?" The guy asked, turning to me.

"Sera." He was tipsy. I could hear it in his voice. Ew. And smell it.

"I've never seen you before." His eyes were big, his tone creepy. Older men always caused knots to fill my stomach. Was this the town's resident drunk? Old Larry had passed when I was in High School. He used to wander the streets on Commercial with a brown paper bag clutched in his right hand.

"Just moved here."

"Why? Why would you want to move here?"

"I grew up here." Chace walked over, interrupting my conversation with my new friend.

"What would you like?"

"I'll take a margarita on the rocks. Salt. Kat will take a frozen strawberry margarita." I could feel the drunk man next to me still ogling me. Chace's eyes had darted over to him a couple times as I was ordering. He left to make our drinks. Shit. Drunky wasted no time.

"So, will I see you around here now that you're settled in?"

"Ah, maybe. It seems like an alright place."

"Well, I will have to buy you a drink some time. Watch my seat. I gotta piss." Chace came back with our drinks as he hopped off. I glared.

"Okay, I didn't know if you needed help there or not." He laughed.

"I needed help! Couldn't you see the look on my face? And he smells like an ashtray."

"He always does, and I thought so, but I didn't want to interrupt if you were into the guy."

"Very funny. No, I am not into older men. Thanks. Next time help me."

"Okay, just give me the look and I'll get the dude gone."

"Thank you, Mr. Bartender. And thank you for these drinks." I raised them and smiled. "I owe you one."

"Yes, you do, and I'm collecting tonight." That was hot; wait, what did he say? I scrunched up my face at him, causing him to chuckle. "I won't be home tonight. Can you make sure my dog, Artax, has food? I would really appreciate it."

"Yeah, yeah, no problem. Anytime. Well I'm going to head back to my table before Smokey the Bear gets back. Thanks."

"Any time." He smiled that small smile again, and turned. I was really beginning to enjoy that smile.

The next couple of weeks in Missouri flew by. Each day I woke around 11:00 to get ready for lunch with Kat. We tried a new restaurant each day. Some of the old ones from years ago were still here, but many new ones had replaced failed establishments. After lunch, I would drop my pal off and head home to check for any of the million packages I ordered. My mother's old closet filled up more each day.

I spent a couple hours on my author Facebook and Twitter pages interacting with fans. I tried my best to ignore the angry comments over not having news about a new novella. After that was taken care of, I changed clothes and headed back into town to meet Kat at her new place.

She decided to be the one to move out of the house she shared with her husband. Her downtown store had a living space above it, a roomy two-bedroom loft apartment. It had been vacant for years and needed a lot of sprucing up. First thing we set our minds to was painting the walls. Kat was sleeping on the couch in the living room, surrounded by boxes. I knew she was glad to have so much work ahead of her. It kept her mind off things. I enjoyed helping her; it kept my mind off the blank screen I still had sitting at home. At least I could pretend it wasn't there for a while.

I knew I was finding new excuses to not write each week, just as I had been doing for over a year, but I wasn't sure how to stop. When I wasn't with Kat, I kept busy in other ways.

I binge watched the entire series of Game of Thrones on DVD. My car got washed every other day. I walked the woods three times. I downloaded 15 audio books. I even did manual labor. I pulled weeds and tulips from the flowerbeds after noticing it on a to-do list Chace had left pinned to the fridge. He thanked me numerous times.

I cleaned the house every other day. I hated cleaning. Although he wasn't there often enough to dirty it, I pitied Chace having to care for large house. Dust settles no matter what. Floors needed sweeping and mopping. Rugs needed vacuuming. The large front porch needed care; dust and dirt were always landing on it. The massive yard was exhausting to upkeep. Having spent so many years in the City, I wouldn't know where to start on any of it. So I kept an eye on Chace's list and phoned my mother when I finished those tasks. Chace asked me not to worry about any of it, that it was his way of paying for room and board, to which I reminded him that I lived there too.

To my shame, after a week and half of all this house upkeep torture, I found someone in the paper to come clean the house. I had a housekeeper in the City. That was more my style.

I saw very little of Chace. I normally woke about an hour before I got out of bed. Mornings were not my favorite, one of the many reasons I didn't emerge until nearly mid-day. I would hear him moving around at 10:00 and then he would leave the house. I wouldn't hear the sound of his jeep making its way back down the drive until nearly midnight.

I wondered when he had free time. I remembered my college days of juggling school and full-time employment.

It had even been quite some time since the last time I heard him play his guitar. A couple of the nights I heard him outside my window playing with his dog before they both came in for the night. He must have felt remorse for leaving him alone for so long. The dog was always on the porch. When I left for lunch, he was there. When I returned, he was there. When I came home at night, he was there, always staring at the driveway.

I found myself staying up until around three in the morning. It was my usual. The later I stayed up, the better I wrote, not that it had helped for a long time. Now I spent the quiet hours simultaneously switching between Facebook, Twitter, my blog, Instagram, and Google. It was a complete waste of time but I couldn't break the cycle. Google was the most depressing. Never Google yourself. There were many articles circulating about me. None of them could stay away from the Tristan topic. Two articles mentioned my exodus from New York. They described how heartbroken I was, and that I left New York to avoid running into my ex.

Tristan was filming in New York, so kudos to the press on that one. I tried not to let it get to me, but being painted the sad, heartbroken woman was not sitting well with me. Not one magazine or newspaper had contacted me to get my side of the story, probably because I changed my number immediately after the breakup. I couldn't control what was written about me but I could control what I said about it, and that had always been nothing.

Kat was my ear through all of this. My life seemed exotic and intriguing to those living here, but I had nothing in common with the friends I had left behind. I was the minority among the females that lived here. I was nearly 30 and had no urge to get married. I did not have baby fever. I think I wanted children one day, but my clock was not ticking, though some would argue that.

I had accomplished so much on my own already; I saw no need to lean on anyone else. Maybe that was why I never found myself in a serious relationship, save for Tristan, the closest I had ever gotten to anything real.

I never felt out of place with these views in New York, but here I felt out of sorts. Despite my lack of warm giggly feelings towards diamond ring commercials, since returning home, I felt the need to find someone. The one-night stands and casual flings needed to stop. Suddenly, I wanted someone who could stay over at my place without me feeling the urge to kick them out at dawn. My relationship with Tristan lasted longer than normal due to the strangeness of it. He was the hottest celebrity of the moment. When I felt suffocated, I could stay home while he was on location. When I craved him, I could fly out to him, once spending two months in Scotland while he filmed. We didn't have to wake to each other every day and go through the standard trials and tribulations of a normal couple.

Possibly, because of my lifestyle, an ordinary relationship was out of the cards. At least that was the excuse I often made for myself. I could write from anywhere. My job was as flexible as it could get. I debated staying here in this small town. My mother would love that. Wait. Why was I even toying with that idea? I escaped this tiny prison years ago. I certainly wasn't going to find anyone to settle down with here. New York was ripe with attractive, smart, successful men. I was here for work. If I planned to take someone seriously, it could wait until I returned to the City.

Whether near or far, my mother called me every day. One weekday I visited her classroom while she took lunch and learned a few things about Chace in the process. I was sitting at one of her student's desks with my feet propped up on another across the aisle when I brought him up.

"So how are things going out at the house?"

"Great. It's been forever since I lived with anyone, although Chace is gone so much, most of the time I feel like I'm living alone."

"Are you two getting along?"

"Yeah," I laughed. "I don't see how anyone could *not* get along with the kid."

"He's a good one. I wish Andrew would, you know, take after him more."

"Yeah, you mentioned that, I know. Maybe he'll figure it out," I shrugged. I hadn't seen my stepbrother since returning home yet. He was up north, in Kansas City with his mother. He wanted to get away after another disagreement with his father. My mother said he would be returning soon. "So, Chace mentioned being out at the house a lot. It sounds like he practically lived with you guys."

"He did. He was like Andrew's brother."

"Why wasn't Chace at his own house much?"

My mother set her fork down. "Well Sera, he had a hard childhood. I thought I told you years ago."

"No, I don't think so," I replied, taking my own lunch from my lap and putting it on the desk.

"It was just Chace and his father at home. I'm glad he was with us so much."

"He wasn't, like, abused or anything was he?"

"No, he wasn't abused."

"Did his dad work nights or something?" I pressed.

"You're awfully curious about him," my mother fished.

I grabbed my salad and brushed it off. "You know me. I ask questions. I'm a writer. Anyways, lunch this Sunday. I'm going to invite Kat."

"Oh, that'd be great. I haven't seen her in forever. How is she doing with everything?"

"I don't know. When I got here I could tell everything had hit her hard. Something is up. The past two days she has been blowing me off. I'm worried about her. I don't know of any other friends she has. She doesn't need to be holed up in that place all alone. It's not good."

"A couple days are nothing. Sometimes you need solitude. And maybe you can get her out here Sunday and things will swing back around the other way."

"I hope."

"Is Chace coming on Sunday too?"

"He hasn't mentioned anything.

"I'll make sure he comes out. If he can get off work. That boy works too much. I told him he could live there for free so he would work less but he insists on working long hours."

"Use your Mom-voice. It always worked on me as a kid." I laughed. "I'm really surprised Andrew is living there with you guys and not out here with Chace. Wouldn't that be the ideal place for a 22-year-old slacker to live?"

My mother rolled her eyes. "Well Andrew got the bright idea that he could live out there with Chace rent free as well. But his dad said he would have to pay rent because he isn't in college."

"Ah, makes sense."

"Now they just drive each other crazy. Andrew with his music, his father with the constant 'get your life together' talk. That's why your brother had to get away for a while. I agree with Paul, he needs to get a plan, but I'd be foolish to believe college is for everyone."

"Mom, you're getting soft," I smirked.

Later that night I replayed the conversation with my mother repeatedly in my head. I still couldn't believe she said that. She shoved college brochures down my throat. I hadn't put up a fight. Poor, Andrew. I hated that he was fighting with his father. I hated that he felt like he needed to run away from his home. I knew the feeling. At least Andrew had a place to run. When I ran away, I didn't have anywhere to go. With Chace's case, it sounded like no one at home cared about him growing up.

In my teens, I might have fantasized about trading places with him. I stared up at the ceiling, on my mother's old bed.

When this house suffocated me, I ran to the woods. I ran to the words trapped within the pages of the journals that littered my room. I loved to run. I learned to cope that way from a young age. I ran away from my mother's questioning eyes on the nights I would cry for no reason. I ran away from the truth, blaming my tears on a sad book I had read, any excuse I could find. I felt a tear run down my cheek, landing on my mother's comforter. I sat up and wiped my eyes. A sound outside my window pulled me from my past. It was the distinct sound of a basketball methodically hitting pavement.

Five

March 25th

I didn't hear Chace pull up the driveway. He must have made it back while I was showering earlier. I needed more friends here. It wasn't like I was writing. I pulled off my robe and searched for warm clothes. The nights still held a chill. I found him outside shooting the ball with his dog relaxing close by on the pavement. I intercepted the ball and he nearly jumped out of his skin at the sight of me.

"Shit! You scared me." He clutched his hand to his chest. "I'm sorry. Were you asleep? Did I wake you up?"

"Nah, I was still up." I couldn't help but grin at his scare. I walked to the edge of the pavement and plopped down, pulling my ankles in close. "Do you normally play basketball by yourself on Friday nights?" I rolled the ball back to him.

"What can I say? I'm a party animal," he joked. "It's been a long ass week. I'm glad it's over." He dribbled the ball around slowly.

"You seem to be a pretty busy guy. Do you ever have free time?"

"Yep, you're looking at it right now."

"So you go to school full time. You have two jobs. And you keep up with the house." I was genuinely impressed.

"Yes, Ma'am. Although you have been helping with that a lot lately. Again. Thank you."

"No big deal." I didn't think he had caught on yet to the fact that I was now paying someone to do the work. "Maybe you should quit one of those jobs."

He raised an eyebrow at me. "Have you been talking to your mom about me?"

"Maybe," I hinted and looked up at the sky, faking innocence.

"Has she recruited you to her side?"

"I don't really have a strong opinion on it. You're young. If you want to burn the candle at both ends, that's your prerogative."

"Well, I am actually considering quitting one of my jobs, so your mom should be happy."

"Mom always knows what's best."

"Your tone implies you know that all too well."

"Oh, growing up her and I would get into so many arguments. I was convinced I was right. I was stubborn. I *am* stubborn. Still, she was always right in the end. I don't regret testing her. And I think she liked that I did, and maybe she wasn't always right. When I decided to go to school in New York she said I would end up back home."

"But, you *are* back home."

"Technicality. Not for good. Just a short while."

"I see."

"I did miss this place though. I didn't realize how much until I got here. It's beautiful. I couldn't sit outside and listen to the crickets at night like this, I couldn't see the stars. There are a million places like this across the Midwest. But it feels different here." The open Ozark air was invigorating. Outside, I didn't feel the ache that house inflicted.

"It's home. I would love to raise a family in a house like this. On land like this."

"You know, you and my brother are so different. I can't believe you two are friends. You seem very mature. You have your priorities together."

"I think Andrew will get it together. Once all of his friends start to settle down and he sees he is the last one acting like a teenager it will kick him in the ass. At least I hope. He has to do it on his own time. No one is going to make him do anything."

"You're right."

"He's a good guy. He would do anything for anyone. He's like family to me."

"Seems like the rest of my family feels that way about you too."

"Yeah. You're step dad is kind of a hard ass though."

"He always has been. I mean, ex-marine-turned-lawyer. What else could he be?"

"True. He didn't really stand a chance." He stopped dribbling and pacing, making his way to me, taking a seat on the pavement as well. I felt nervous at his nearness.

"The way he looks at my mom, though. He's never a hard ass with her. What are your parents like?" I couldn't help but ask. I hadn't learned enough from my mother.

"Ah, well. I just have my dad. He lives up in Saint Louis. I was born there, and once I graduated high school, he went back up there. I try to get up and see him when I can."

"Any siblings?"

"No." He twirled the ball in front of him, focused on it.

"Well I know what it's like to be the only child."

"Did your father ever have any other kids?"

"No. He didn't even want to have me."

"What?" He turned to me, away from the ball spinning in his hands.

"I always asked my mom about my father. She never wanted to tell me anything, so I invented stories in my mind. All of my friends had families that were whole, ya know?"

Chace nodded like he understood what I was saying all too well. "It took me a while to realize how lucky I was to have the mother I do. We were an odd household, with my grandparents here. It wasn't what some would consider to be a 'normal family.' Eventually, when I was around 17, I got her to confess."

"What happened?" Chace asked me, leaning back on his elbows, looking up at me.

"My mother met my father her freshman year of college. He was a senior. When she graduated, he proposed. She said yes. It wasn't until after they made their vows that he admitted that he didn't want to have children. He had misled her. She took her vows seriously and promised to love him forever. She felt cheated. According to my mom, he had agreed that children would be in their future before they wed.

When my mother turned 31, she couldn't take it anymore. She desperately wanted to have a child. Despite his begging, she filed for divorce. He fought to keep her. Promised her the world, but the one thing he couldn't promise was all she desired. After my mother moved back in with her parents, she learned of her pregnancy. When she told her estranged husband the news, he stopped begging for reconciliation. He no longer wanted her back. He didn't want to be a father. He confessed that if she hadn't filed for divorce, he would have after she revealed she was pregnant."

I had never told anyone this story before, not even to Kat. I looked down into Chace's eyes. They were the reason for my confession.

"What a fool." He didn't need to say anything else.

"I don't even know why I am blabbing about all of this." I never opened up to strangers, I barely opened up to those I held close, but here I was doing just that.

"I don't mind."

"I've never talked to anyone about this."

"Sometimes it's easy to tell someone you don't know very well the things it's harder to tell those tied closest to you." Was this guy in my brain?

"Do you have a girlfriend?" I couldn't stop myself. I thought back to my first day here when that pretty girl got into his jeep once he dropped me off at Kat's shop.

"No. Not anymore. Recently single. Does it look like I have time for one?"

"You must have a ton of girls your age chasing you."

"I've never actually had a serious girlfriend before. If you don't have time for someone you shouldn't be in a relationship. No one wants a half-assed boyfriend. My ex ended up resenting me because I never took her anywhere. I just never had any time. I knew it would happen so it was my fault really."

"She was hot, huh?"

"You are correct in that assumption," he laughed. "That's what got me. A pretty face can turn a man to goo sometimes."

"Well if you quit that job you will have more time on your hands."

"I don't know." He sat up and tossed the basketball in front of him, we both watched it roll over to the grass. He leaned back on his elbows again.

I turned to him. "Would she be willing?"

"Yes."

"Whoa, no hesitation there." I leaned back as well. "Has she mentioned it?"

"She comes up to the bar a lot. Her eyes. It's there."

"You're a heart breaker."

"No. No, not true," he laughed, softly. "So, do you miss it?"

"Miss what?"

"The City?"

"Yes and no." He hopped up at my answer, startling me.

"I'm going to get a beer. Do you want anything?"

"Wine. I need wine." He returned quickly, handing me a glass of Merlot.

"How much traveling do you do with your job?"

"A lot lately it seems. When you mix in the promotion I did for the books and then the traveling for the movies, that's a lot of frequent flyer miles."

"I'd love to travel."

"Have you been anywhere?"

"Not since I was a kid, really. Well, no, about two years ago I drove down to Nashville for the weekend with your brother.

"Oh, I like Nashville."

"I'd live there."

"Do you think that when you graduate you will teach here?" Though he mentioned raising a family here, I could see him leaving. I could see him doing anything he desired.

"I haven't really decided yet."

"Well, you have time. What two years left?"

"Yep."

"What made you want to become a teacher? Please don't say my mom."

"Your mom." We both laughed.

"So, her persuasion worked on you then. She tried with me."

"Nah, she didn't have to say anything to me. I think I knew for a long time, but never admitted it. The two years after high school where I just goofed off, it wasn't really at the surface of my mind. I did great in school, I really thrived there. Sometimes that's the only place a kid can be around people who truly care. Your mom was one of them. I'd love to be that to someone too."

"Like Aiden."

"Yeah, like Aiden."

"I'm glad my mom has you around to help out." I glanced around at the flowers and greenery surrounding the driveway.

"I owe her a lot. So, did you always know you wanted to be a writer?"

"Yes. I just never expected to make any money. Or to be writing in the genre I am."

"Would you ever write anything else?"

"It's hard to switch once you have a solid fan base that expects a certain product from you." I thought of all the magical places my writing took me as a child and during high school. I missed it. I missed the creative freedom. My words had become a burden.

"You can do anything you want," he encouraged. "Even if it seems scary, it doesn't mean it isn't worth a try."

"Yeah, I guess." I took another sip of my wine.

"Don't let fear sway you. You're not your past."

His words felt like a knife. They slipped between my rib bones and nestled in with the poisonous parts. If he only knew. "So do you ever write anything besides music? Do you ever write lyrics?" I wanted to hear him play again. My balcony was cold without his guitar below it.

"Ah, yes. But never for anyone else's ears." He crossed one arm over his eyes.

"Why?" I turned on my side, facing him.

"I don't know. I just couldn't imagine someone else singing my words, and expressing feelings that belong to me. But, I have been thinking of letting Andrew do a couple of my songs at a show soon. Maybe. It's scary, you know?"

"Yes, I completely understand that. It's hard to be vulnerable in that way. And for all I know, you write crappy songs." I did not believe this for a second. But I was enjoying the back and forth between us.

"This is true."

"I find that hard to believe though."

"Why's that?" He removed his arm and looked up at me.

"You have the face. The 'I-write-lyrics-that-make-women-swoon' face."

"I didn't even know that was a thing!" He laughed. It was a beautiful laugh. His laugh was music.

"It is. I just created it." I lied down next to him. It felt too strange to be leaning over him like that. Like I was hitting on him.

"Well, the best songs come from sadness. And I don't think your brother's band wants to sing songs like that."

"You like country music, don't you? All sad sappy songs?" I never listened to country music once I moved away. Lately I was surrounded by it again.

"They aren't all sad. But yes, country music is home to the most meaningful sad songs."

"Well, you don't come off as a sad guy at all. So I will just say yes, you write swoon-worthy music."

"If you're trying to get me to sing a song I wrote to prove you wrong, it won't work."

I shrugged. "Can't blame me for trying, Sir."

"I think you're adopted."

"What!? Why?" I rolled on my side again, nearly knocking my wine glass over. Chace quickly grabbed it, and then set it in the grass. He stared at the sky, never turning to me.

"Your mom is the sweetest woman in the world. You're mischievous."

"Am not," I pouted.

"Yes you are. This is the first I've seen it. But it's definitely there."

"Whatever. You've barely been around since I moved in."

"You're shy, but once you get a glass of wine in you, watch out!"

"Ah, this is true. Okay the wine is mischievous. I am an angel."

"I like it." He still wouldn't look at me.

"Thanks." I made myself lie on my back again. Perhaps I was making him nervous. "So, my mom said that this Sunday she would like to have lunch over here, or at her house, I can't remember. She says she needs to take another look at the landscaping. So yeah, here." The wine was making me fuzzy.

"Yeah, she texted me that too. About an hour ago."

"You want to help me take care of the food?"

"Yeah, I can do that. Anything in particular you have in mind?" He stretched his arms out and nestled them under his head.

"Mexican."

"What exactly?"

"Nacho bar, and I make these amazing steak tacos."

He leaned up and tipped the last of his beer back and set the bottle on the pavement. I found myself watching his movements. The wine was doing bad things to my brain. He turned and caught me staring, returning my gaze with a shy smile. "Want to see something?" He asked, standing. So I nodded. He offered his hand, and I grabbed it. His touch was not helping. I dropped his hand as soon as I was on my feet.

I followed him to the shed on the other side of the house. Upon reaching it, he slipped a small key from his pocket. Growing up, my grandfather had always kept this building locked. I had not been in it since I returned. The hair on the back of my neck stood up. I reached up, rubbing my nerves away.

I followed him in, curiosity pushing my anxiety away. He flipped the light on and there was no question what he intended to show me. The shop was littered with bicycles. It was too much to take in all at once. My eyes rapidly scanned. Some were new, some old. Some rusted, some with brand new paint. Some were cruisers, some road bikes, some mountain bikes. I saw a tandem bike in the far corner. They were all so beautiful. The collection was amazing. My eyes came back to Chace, who was bouncing on the seat of an older model bike that had been restored. Candy apple red.

He smiled at me. "I have a problem, huh?"

"No. It's awesome. When did you start buying them?"

"High school. It's become an obsession. Honestly it's part of the reason I have so many jobs. This hobby is not cheap. I should just sell some of them and take a semester or two off from working. It would be easier. But I can't part with any of them."

My mother had been the same way growing up with typewriters. She had tons and could never resist when we found one at an antique mall. I loved them, too. They were so beautiful. She left many behind. They were never just for looks. She used them. She let me use them. "Do you ride all of these bikes?"

"I try to get all of them in running condition. If not, those are the ones I sell. They aren't appealing to me if I can't ride them."

"How often do you ride?"

"Every week from spring until winter."

I recalled the bike rack on the back of his jeep. I myself had not been on a bike in years. When I was a kid, I desperately wanted a teal mountain bike. I had seen one at Wal-Mart and it was love at first sight. My mother and I had ventured to the store in her small car, so taking it home along with the groceries was not an option. At dinner that night I talked incessantly about the bike. I wanted one of those little license plates on the back with my name. I begged to return to the store to purchase it.

My grandfather told me that he had a perfectly good bike in the shed I could use. He could give it a new paint job and it would be good as new. Of course, this was not an even trade in my young eyes. I wanted the shiny new one at the store. Many of my friends had new bikes of their own. I never got a bike that year, but my grandfather worked on the old Schwinn in the garage. Out of guilt. Hush money.

The next spring he had our mile long driveway paved. Some might have thought it a waste of money, but my grandmother wanted somewhere to walk, and driving into town each day to circle the park was a pain. My desire for a bike came back just as he was finishing his restoration. He had installed a new seat, and a basket. The body was painted sea foam green, and a new set of tires were put on. It was beautiful. I loved it.

I would ride back and forth down the drive each night, passing my grandmother and saying to her in a sing-song voice "I'm faster than yyooouuuu!" She would laugh at me and wave me on. When I went off to college, I reminded my mother repeatedly that my bike was to never be sold. The memories I shared with my grandmother were tethered to it. I didn't know where it was now.

Six

March 27th

Sunday brought with it beautiful weather. Ideal for the get together at noon. I took a couple Advil PMs the night before to ensure I would fall asleep at a decent hour to rise early and assist Chace. My mother would be coming over, as well as Paul, who I had not seen yet since making it home. He worked often.

My mom remarried the summer after I graduated high school. She had been engaged to Paul for two years, and they didn't live together until after their vows. It was a strange thing to do in these times, but my mother didn't want to move me out of the house we shared with her parents so late in my high school years. I should have told her it would have been a relief.

Paul treated my mother like a queen, and was always caring towards me. His son was very important to him. He wasn't a part-time father. He shared custody of Andrew with his ex-wife. I didn't get to spend much time with Andrew back then, between our parents living in separate houses, and the time he spent at his own mother's, but I loved him. He was a hyper child and made me laugh. I knew early on that he would be like a flesh and blood brother to me. I was happy he would be coming over today too. I had never seen him interact with Chace. I was curious about their friendship. They were so different.

Chace had Aiden over. Another relationship I was curious about. I could hear them downstairs in the kitchen as I applied my makeup and fixed my hair. I loved the sounds of the house now. Maybe I could stitch up my wounds with these new sounds.

My opened balcony door allowed for a breeze to enter. Being back here reminded me I didn't need a regular family. The first stories I wrote were all different ways my childhood could have been with a loving father around. After finding out he played no part in my life, the stories changed.

I wondered how and if we would ever meet, and if our relationship could just start anew. Other nights, I fantasized about telling him off. Screaming at him about how he was a horrible father, and that I had a new and better dad. When I began writing poetry, many pieces were about him. I never let my mother read them. I feared she would blame herself, and I never wanted to cause her pain. No other mother, in my eyes, could be her. I wrote about him to exorcise him from my mind. Certainly, he had forgotten about me long ago.

Now here Chace was, all of 22, being a positive male figure in the life of a child. I found the two boys around the kitchen island, chopping vegetables. Chace, working on his own pile, darted his eyes over to Aiden every couple of seconds. The child's hold on his knife perfectly matched his mentor.

"Need any help?" I wanted to be useful. In a real way, not in a way I could buy. Chace stopped chopping and waved me over.

"Can you finish with this? I'll go out back and start pulling the patio furniture out of the shed." He handed the knife over to my reluctant hands. I was a lousy cook with only a few go-to recipes to turn to. Surely I could handle what he had left.

Once Chace headed outside, I walked over to the small radio on the counter and began switching stations. I found a country station playing Garth Brooks and immediately stopped. I knew every hit he put out, thanks to my mother. I remembered her excitement when he came out of retirement. I turned back to the counter and Aiden's unimpressed face.

"You like country too? That's all Chace listens to in the car. I hate it." He scrunched up his nose and shook his head animatedly.

"New country is horrible. This is old country." I knew every 90's country hit by heart. My mother would blast it in the summers when we would ride into town to pick up groceries. The windows would be down and our hair would whip in the wind as we sang at the top of our lungs.

"That's what he says. I don't like any of it."

"How about we finish this song then you can pick a station. Deal?"

"Deal," he said, smiling, and returned to the task at hand. My phone dinged. It was Kat.

Kat: What should I bring today? What time again?
Me: Just whatever you want to drink. Noon.
Me: No, wait, bring tortilla chips. And an extra sour cream. You can never have enough.
Kat: Sounds good. See ya soon.

Chace walked back in as I set my phone back down. He raised an eyebrow at me and my small pile of vegetables.

"Sorry," I muttered. "I'm not a fast chopper." He playfully waved me away from the cutting board. I walked around to the bar stool and sat.

"Aiden, why don't you go outside and get Artax? Bring him inside. He needs a bath before people start coming over and petting him. Use the downstairs bathroom. His shampoo is already down there." The child sprinted off at full speed. Chace laughed. "I'm glad I have today off for this."

"So why do you work so much anyways? Other than to buy a million bicycles. Do you have a big payment on your jeep or something?" I was glad he was here too.

"No, that was a high school graduation present from my father," he answered, flatly.

"Oh." I didn't want to ask more about his family. Lie. I did want to, but I was afraid. I had learned a little through my mother and through him the night before. But I hadn't pressed. When Chace was near, I felt off. He was this strange mystery. I wanted to read him. I wanted to know his secrets.

"I want to take the summer off. From school and from work. I want to hang with Aiden when school lets out. His mom is working two jobs and going to school full-time. I don't want him to just go to some babysitter's house all day. She doesn't have family around for him."

"That's, that's amazing." His heart. It was something beautiful. Men his age, unattached, didn't want to do these things. They wanted to have fun, and be free.

"Nah."

"No, it is," I affirmed. "This kid isn't your family. I'm assuming you don't want any money to watch him. Correct?"

"No."

"You're doing something wonderful." I knew he was aware of this. It was the reason he was doing it. Because it was the right thing to do. He was not the type to tell someone to receive attention. He did it simply because he was good. I wanted to be good the way he was good. I was grim grey toned morals and sin, someone who wore bruises since they were 10-years-old.

"Thanks. He needs a man in his life. Someone to set a good example. Someone he can count on." Poor male figures broke little boys just as easily as little girls.

"You're going to be a great dad one day." If only my father

had been that kind of man. How would I have turned out? Would my life have been the way my silly stories described? It was no use to wonder. I had this life and I did not need him. I had proven that time and time again.

"Yeah, maybe in five or ten years. Not until I'm completely stable and ready."

"So you're not in a hurry like every other kid your age around here?"

"No, definitely not. I want to do a lot of things before I start a family. I have a lot of places I would like to travel. Like you have. There is this huge world out there away from this town. You know that better than most. I want to see it."

"You said you could raise a family here one day, but have you ever thought about moving away? You mentioned Nashville. Anywhere else you could see yourself?"

"Saint Louis is another possibility, it's where my dad and aunts are. But I'm not close with any of them. I'm close with your family. I'd move for them sooner than my own."

"I'm sorry."

"Don't be," he insisted. "Family is important to me; it just isn't a priority to the one I was born into anymore. Things happen. People grow apart, or are torn apart." He stopped chopping vegetables and went to the sink to wash his hands.

"I know. I do miss my family. I fly my mom out every summer and holidays." I felt a little guilty for not being there more for the family he loved so much. I just couldn't bring myself to face this house until now.

"I always wondered about the daughter who never came home," he said as he turned back to me, smirking.

"Yeah, I know. Kind of shitty of me. I just figured giving them a chance to visit New York was a better option than me coming back to this tiny town. I really have no excuse though."

"What's the hardest part of your job?"

"Book signings." There was no question about that.

"Really? Why?"

"There's never enough time. Before I sold the rights to the books, my singings were smaller, more intimate. I was able to really talk with each reader. They would last hours and I would feel like I was there for just a moment. Now, it's insane. Don't get me wrong, I am so grateful for my success, but most of the time I only have time to sign a book and take a photo. I know that upsets people, and I really don't blame them. Some fans drive from hours away. I just wish I had more time to give. I try to throw a little bit of goodness out there to make up for it. I do big prizes at the events."

"I'm sure they appreciate that."

"I guess," I shrugged. "I just hate letting anyone down and after each singing I get emails expressing disappointment. I've done more signings recently though despite not having any new material. I figured since I can't write I should get out there a bit and see people."

"That's good of you. You shouldn't be so hard on yourself. You can't help the fact that you have too many fans to make the time to talk to each and every single one of them."

"Thanks." It didn't feel like enough sometimes.

"You're living the dream aren't you?"

"I am very fortunate. Sitting in my tree house scribbling away on my spiral notepad, who would have thought it would end up this way?" All this success for writing that wasn't from the heart. It felt like the biggest lie of all. It had been luck. Chance. I didn't deserve it. Would I have been a hit with my poetry? Probably not. I stared at my hands on the counter in front of me. Who was I? Someone living a borrowed life?

"I'm sure anyone who picked up your work could have guessed."

"Maybe I'm a horrible writer. I doubt you have read anything." I wanted to joke with him. I wanted to pull myself from the ugly feelings that had crept inside my head.

"You don't think I read your books?" He cocked his head to the side, coming around the island to where I sat on the barstool.

"There's no way you do." I turned in my seat to face him. No way did he read my stuff. No freakin' way. All of my sin and debauchery, the thought of his eyes on it made me blush. He was pure and all things good. I was the devil sitting in this kitchen with him.

"Maybe I do read lady porn. You don't know me."

"What have you read?" Say all of it. Say none of it.

"Everything." He didn't smile. He simply stared into my eyes. He didn't blink.

"Quit messing with me." I hopped off the stool, warm from his gaze. I went to the refrigerator and kneeled inside to get the orange juice out.

"I'm not."

I popped back up and looked at him over the door. "For real?"

"This whole town has probably read them! Even the ones who like to bad mouth the books. You're my best friend's sister. You're the famous writer who emerged from our tiny town, the only one besides Mikey Finn to do something extraordinary."

"Mikey Finn?" I wanted to change the subject. Desperately.

"He graduated a couple years ahead of me. He's in the NFL now."

"Oh wow, that's great." I shut the refrigerator door and turned away from him.

"Yeah, quit trying to distract me from complimenting you. You're a great writer."

"Thank you, Chace. I can't believe you read the books." I pulled a glass from the cabinet and began pouring.

"Well, it's not like I carried them around to class with me. I'd never live that down. But, you have this huge library here. And your mom has all of your books in it." He walked over to me and pulled a glass out for himself. "Can you pour me some, too?"

"Sure."

"Thanks."

"In New York, space is a hot commodity. My apartment is pretty roomy, and I have a library there, just not like this one. I send books here all the time."

"Was that room always so big?"

"No, my grandparent's room was directly above the study. I had mom hire someone to take the floor out. To put in floor-to-ceiling shelving and ladders."

"It's awesome. You've never thought of coming back here to live?"

"No, never."

"I see." His mouth turned up slightly when he said it.

"Why?"

"I remember what it looked like before you made the best-sellers list for the first time. You've had a lot of work done out here since then."

"I like to spend money," I shrugged. I had to change this house. I had to rip it apart and start new. I would do it one day. One room at a time.

"Yes, I know you like to spend money. I've noticed all the packages being delivered."

"I collect clothes the way you do bikes."

"I love those bikes!"

"How many can you ride at once?" This had become our thing. Teasing one another. I loved the friendship that was forming.

"One. Not relevant though. Each serves its own purpose."

"Mmm hmm."

"You should go riding with me some time."

"I don't have a bike." I had decided, before popping my Advil last night that I needed a road bike to ride with Chace. I jumped online and began researching. I decided to make an appointment at the nearest bike shop.

"I know someone who does."

"You have men's bikes."

"No, I have others. I have a couple girls' bikes. And you're short enough they would probably be perfect for you."

"So why cycling?

"It's easier on your joints than running." He seemed slightly embarrassed with this answer. I couldn't imagine why, but something was suddenly on the outskirts of my mind. Something I should know about him. I felt as though he thought I knew more about him than I did. I was such a selfish creature. What had I been told about him in the past? He had been Andrew's best friend for years. My mother surely brought him up on the phone from time to time. What was I missing? I would ask her when she showed up today.

March 27th

The house quickly filled with the kind of loud noises I loved in these walls; laughter and the bustle of moving bodies. My mother and her husband showed up a half hour early, as usual. My brother, back in town, showed up a half hour late, as usual. Kat, some of my mother's friends, as well as Andrew's band members stopped over too. They were a fun bunch. I missed my grandmother's presence.

The boys, sans Chace, started up a game of volleyball in the back yard, pulling the net from the shop building. My stepfather and Kat even joined in. It was nice to see them let loose. My mother, along with her friends and I, watched from lawn chairs. I did not have aunts and uncles, but I had many stand-ins. My mother had numerous friends, mostly teachers. They were as warm and intelligent as she was. I could go to any of them with a problem.

Surprisingly, my mother did lose one friend when my first book was published. She was very religious, and had strong opinions about my work. My mother, of course, defended me. The relationship became strained, and eventually died. I felt bad. I felt to blame. She assured me that I was not. I was lucky to have these strong women sitting next to me. Kat was as well.

Kat never had a positive female figure in her life. Her mother chose meth over family. My friend spent a lot of time at our house. My mother was forever taking care of children, in and out of school. Much like Chace with Aiden.

He had taken the boy to play baseball, past the volleyball madness. I was very sure Kat would be a wonderful mother one day. Yet, I was never sure of myself. I was not like my mother. I was not like Kat or Chace.

I was not outgoing and warm, not since I was young. I did not have an easy way with children. I was a loner. I was selfish. Friends had suggested this was why I feared commitment. To avoid family. To avoid being selfless. They always suggested it in a nice way.

I pushed my insecurities aside and took in my surroundings again. Kat was staring adamantly at her phone, furiously typing. I wondered who she was texting, and hoped it was not her ex. Her flushed neck made me think it was, and perhaps he was starting an argument with her. I cleared my throat to get her attention. Her eyes flew to me. I mouthed "you okay?" and she nodded. I didn't believe her. But I wouldn't press. I motioned for her to come into the house with me and she did. I grabbed the nearly empty lemonade container on my way. "Are we still on for lunch tomorrow?" I asked as I reached the fridge.

"Yeah. Where do you want to eat? Peppers?"

"No, I'm not in the mood for Mexican," I answered, finding a Cheshire grin on her face. "What?"

"How are you going to live with that guy and not fool around with him?"

"Chace? What do you mean?"

"You know what I mean."

"Like I've said a million times, he is just too young. Look at him out there. He is like family." It was in my mind. She didn't need to plant it there. It wasn't simply because of his looks, which were amazing, but his heart was getting to me. I wanted it.

I wanted mine to be somewhat near its size.

"He is like family to *your* family. Not to *you*. You've been gone. And it's not like he is a kid. Hell, your brother isn't a kid anymore."

"Kat, shut it. Are you hinting that you think Andrew is hot? 'Cause, yuck."

"He is! Sorry." She shrugged her shoulders.

"Kill me now." I made a gun with my finger and placed it at my temple.

"I'm not saying I'm going to hit on your brother. I'm just saying," she paused, "I know age won't be an issue for you if you get some wine in you."

I hated hearing that. Not because it wasn't true, but because it was a part of me I wanted to leave behind. The promiscuity. The recklessness. I didn't want to sleep with Chace; I wanted to be more like him. More like Kat. More like my mother. Not like Andrew. Ha. I just didn't want to be me anymore. Kat saw the change in my face. I always wore my emotions on them. I couldn't hide.

"I'm sorry, Sera," she apologized. "I didn't mean it in a bad way. You just do what you want. You live in the moment. There's nothing bad about that."

"I don't want to be that way anymore. I just want to be here and write again. I want to be here for you. See my family more. Let's face it, I haven't been the best friend, daughter, or sister. I never come home. I should have come home. I'm that person who gets rich and forgets where she came from. And look how beautiful it is." I looked out the window. The land was beautiful. The trees kept my secrets. All of my guilt was catching up to me. I was surrounded by everything that mattered today. All the things that should matter to a person.

"You didn't forget us," she assured me. "You called all the time. Not a week went by when you didn't text. And look at this house. You have helped keep it beautiful. I think you knew you would come back. I think we all did." I guess Chace wasn't the only one who thought I had been renovating this house because I would return. They were off. *So off.*

"Maybe you knew something I didn't. I never saw it."

"You know what I know? I know today is great. It's because you're home. Look at us all out there. We love you."

"I love you so much."

"I know," she said, reaching for me. I hated hugs, but I needed hers. She needed me more than I needed her but once again, she was being the mothering kind. She was taking care of me when her life was falling apart.

I dried my tears and headed back outside with Kat. To my surprise, she was able to get me to join in a volleyball game. I was horrible. The rest of the day went by quickly. When my mother and Paul left, they hugged me tight. They did the same with Chace. After helping me clean, he left to take Aiden home. He was barely out of the driveway when he texted me to not get ready for bed. He wanted to have a beer on the deck.

I felt a rush at this, followed by guilt. I stamped it down and found a bottle of wine. A half hour later, his jeep lights lit up the drive as I sat reclined on the back deck. He went inside, grabbed a beer and joined me. It didn't take much small talk before he asked me about my ex. It startled me. I was not expecting it. This was something men generally did when they were interested in a woman. I was such a presumptuous idiot.

"What was it like dating a celebrity?" He took a swig of his beer.

"Weird. Different. The same." I had been asked this so many times. I never knew how to answer, honestly.

"How? Explain it to me. If you don't mind, I mean."

"The weird: people in the street waiting for us to leave a restaurant so they can get a picture. I didn't like it. Being a successful author isn't in the same realm as being a successful actor or musician. I didn't sign up for it. So we went to great lengths to avoid the public. No enjoying the outside patio of our favorite bistro on a summer day. It felt like something was being taken from me.

The different: I was with someone who was as passionate about something as I was. His career was as dear to him as mine is to me. It had been a while since I cared about anyone who didn't seem to just be drifting through life, or had a job that just paid the bills but didn't ignite passion. I was avoiding the thing I was most passionate about the entire year he was in my life. I wanted to pretend he could be the filler of my void." I felt my old feelings flare up. Tristan was like me in so many ways, which could have been the reason for our failure. One among many.

"And the same?"

"The same: we drifted. He lied, I avoided. He left. I didn't cry." And that had bothered him.

"So it ended pretty mutually?"

"Yes and no. I went to this cabin that I write at sometimes. I told him I needed the weekend to focus and to get my head on straight. About the middle of the next week, I got a text from my best friend in New York saying I needed to check out People Magazine's website. I found an article saying Tristan had ended his year long relationship with the author. It wasn't the first time I had seen something false about me in the media, but the picture of him kissing his co-star from the new film he was working on was undeniable.

It could have been an on-set photo, but he was wearing a shirt I bought him. I didn't even get a chance to grab my phone and call him. Someone must have told him about the article too. He just texted me 'sorry,' nothing else. No explanation, no denial. I knew I should call him and cuss him out or cry, or throw something, but I didn't respond. I went back to the City and found him at my door. He looked sad, but not guilty.

He told me he had never been in a relationship where he felt alone. He said he had fallen for me before our first kiss. Every day he saw me on set, completely passionate about the books and the film. He would watch me take notes or write. It was beautiful to him. But I had not written a word since that first kiss. He couldn't be the reason I had writer's block. Because I wasn't who he fell for. I was distracted, and aloof. He wanted me to fall in love with it all again."

"He sounds like a coward to me."

"Yeah, he just wanted to screw that chick." I tipped back the last of my glass and laughed.

"Thank God." His voice was so relieved. "I really thought from the way you were telling me how he explained himself that you felt you were to blame."

"No. It was a chicken shit move. The way he let himself be photographed out in the open like that, the way we were so skilled at avoiding. It was obviously deliberate. I still don't understand why he explained himself at all when he could have left it alone after knowing I saw them."

"Well Chicken Shit felt guilty about the chicken shit move."

"I guess so," I considered. "But I was pretty aloof with him. I think it pissed him off more than anything that I never cried. What about you? Tell me more about that hot ex of yours."

"Ah, Caroline," he opened. "I don't know if she even counts as an ex."

"What do you mean?"

"We only dated for about a month. So who was the boyfriend before Mister Movie Star?"

"Ah, no one really. Not since college." I reached for the throw blanket at my feet and wrapped it around my arms. I felt warm from the wine but the goosebumps on my arms were telling.

"I don't believe that." There was a flirtatious tone to his voice.

"It's true. I spend a lot of time alone. Nothing is stable. It can be, but I guess I like the change. Once I moved to Austin Texas for three months just to get out of the City and write from a new environment and perspective. It's not exactly the easiest life for relationships. So I tend to always keep them casual."

"I see. So what was college boyfriend like?"

"Casual," I laughed. "We weren't serious. And he is actually the man to credit for my career."

"What do you mean?"

"Oh, I regret this conversation." I threw my arm over my eyes and bit my lip. Chace reached over and pulled my arm away. His finger lightly ran across the tattoo on my forearm. *A kiss may ruin a human life.* Oscar Wilde. I said it twice in my head before pulling away quickly.

"Come on, tell me." He laid his hand in his lap. I saw his knuckles tighten.

"No, I don't want to now."

"You can't leave it like that! I'll go nuts wondering what that meant! Was he a college professor who discovered your writing? Something like that?"

"No, no. Not that tired old cliché. He was a senior like me."

"Your face is so red. You don't have to tell me."

"No, I'm going to. Okay, um. He and I had a great sex life. We didn't hold back from each other. It was fun. He knew I loved to write. So, he uh, he said I should write about our sex. So I did." This was going into dangerous territory.

"I wasn't expecting that…"

"I wrote up a little story about how we met, and everything about us. We had fun with it. I gave it to him and he loved it. He said I should try to publish it. I was not okay with that. He eventually convinced me to; I changed our names and everything. I just posted it online and it blew up."

"And now you're a best-selling author."

"Yep."

"Do you still talk to him?"

"Ah, about twice a year we will email."

"This is a really weird conversation." He stood and pointed at my glass. I handed it to him.

"Yeah, I was trying to avoid that." It was too easy to talk to him; he brought it out of me. He retreated into the house to refill our drinks and returned quickly.

"Do you turn red every time you tell that story?" I reached for the half-full glass in his hand.

"I don't tell that story. I just say it all comes from my imagination. Every book."

"So, they all come from real life?" He turned to me, eyes burning into my profile.

"Yeah..." This was not something I told anymore. I could count the people who knew this on one hand.

"I see."

"I bet you are thinking about them now right? My books..." Why did he have to tell me he read them? I shouldn't have admitted this. My dark truth. I felt cheap. I was the demon in my own life. Loneliness didn't seek me out. I hunted it down.

"How many people know you write about your real life sex life?" Artax ran up the steps to Chace and laid his head on his owner's outstretched legs. He reached down to pet the dog lovingly behind his ears.

"My assistant. My college boyfriend. My best friend in New York." My therapist. The unlucky four.

"That's it?" His blue eyes still burned into my side. Now I was the one avoiding his gaze as he did mine on the pavement two nights before.

"Yeah. And now you..." I tipped back my second glass of wine. I felt dizzy and warm. I felt a certain relief as well. I was telling a man I knew only a short time more than I had told Kat and it felt great.

"How long has it been since you wrote? You said a year?"

"Longer." I hated the reminder. I didn't need it. It was

etched on my skin. It felt nearly as permanent as the ink covering my surface.

"So you haven't had sex in over a year?"

"No, I've had sex. Tristan and I only split, what, a month ago?" Our sex had been amazing. It had been worth writing about.

"So, why the block?"

"I'm over it, I guess." I was over it before the madness had begun.

"Over writing?"

"No, I love to write, but I want more. I want to write a *real* novel. With no sex. I don't want to write anymore synonyms for 'cock'!" He nearly spit his beer. I finally turned to him.

"Oh, is that all?"

"I want to write the way I did when I was a kid. The way I did in high school and college before this whole crazy train left the station." I had forgotten what that even looked like. I needed to find my old journals.

"I bet anything you write is great."

"Thanks." He had only read my novellas. He wouldn't know. I wanted him to know.

"Why'd you tell me all of this?"

"You're very easy to talk to," I admitted, "I can see why you have so many friends, and why my family loves you. The kids you teach are going to take one look at your face and know they can trust you with any secret they have." I felt like I could as well.

Eight

April 1st

Tick...
Tock...
Tick...
Tock...
Shut...
The...
Fuck...
Up.

I was going to smash my watch. How could it be that loud from across the room? Another five days had gone by in Missouri with no writing. I was staring at a lonely Friday night.

I had been so busy so the week flew by. Lunches with Kat, dinners at my mothers. I had probed her about Chace. I knew I was missing something about him. It nagged at me. When she finally told me, my memory awoke as well and I remembered his story before she had even finished. How could I have forgotten his story? It was tragic. I would look at him differently. Not in a bad way. There had been very little sight of Chace. Another busy week took him from home.

He texted me a few times, asking favors to do with his dog. I welcomed the tiny things he asked of me. Now, though, the house was too quiet. The desire to close my laptop and turn on the television burned me. I took my phone off the nightstand again, no texts or calls. Kat and my mother were asleep most likely, my best friend in New York was on a date, and Chace wasn't home. He should be getting off work soon.

I couldn't text him or go down stairs when he got back for company. Did we know each other well enough for me to do that? Barely a week ago we discussed my sex life and I divulged a secret Kat didn't even know.

I drafted a text to him. Then deleted it. Then drafted one again. Then deleted it. Why was my isolation bothering me? I was no stranger to it. I went on writing retreats all the time.

I flinched at the sound of Artax's bark. Chace was home. The gravel crunched as I stilled myself in the dark of my room, my face illuminated by the screen of my Macbook. I slowly closed it. Maybe he would play guitar on the porch tonight, it would cap off this horrible, wordless day nicely. I melted into the pillow behind me, listening to Chace talk softly to his dog on the porch below, suddenly my phone alerted in my hand. A text from him.

Chace: I hope you didn't fall asleep with that door open.

I glanced at my balcony door smiling. I texted back that I was awake. I would never go to sleep with the door open.

Chace: Do you own a bathing suit?
Me: No??
Chace: Are you unsure if you do?
Me: I don't.
Chace: Dang, I figured one had to be in one of the million boxes delivered here. Do you have anything to swim in?
Me: What? Why? It's midnight. We don't own a pool.
Chace: I've had a shitty day. I wanted to see you in a bath-

ing suit.

    Me: Um...

    Chace: Kidding! Just trust me. It'll be fun

    Me: Okay. Only because of your shitty day.

    Chace: Meet me outside in a bit!

I met Chace outside by his jeep. He was kneeling by his dog, ruffling his fur. He had on a pair of dark grey running pants, a tight white t shirt, and a pair of eye glasses. Those were new. Attractive. Not going to lie. He stood at my approach and shrugged at my clothes. "You look properly attired for breaking and entering."

I halted my steps. "What?"

"Nothing. Hop in!" He was energetic and alive.

I choked out a breath, half laughing at his playfulness. "I believe I heard the words 'breaking and entering.' No way am I getting in that jeep." I crossed my arms over my chest for emphasis.

"Trust me. We are going to have fun. I can't go alone." He walked over to his vehicle and swung the door open, hopping in.

"To where?" I sounded like an old lady as I begrudgingly followed. I opened my door and pursed my lips as I stood outside, staring at his blue eyes.

He lost his smile, and stared up at the sky for a moment, then moved his eyes to me. "I've had a horrible day."

"Me too." I needed inspiration. I needed more than the glow of a handful of Apple products. I had a slight ache in my right temple from the stress of it all. It always happened when I stared at a screen for too long with still hands.

"Then get in." The moonlight reflected off his glasses and my resolve vanished. We pulled out of the driveway and headed away from town. I was unfamiliar with what was in this direction. Having no friends or family living further down our road, I never explored. My mother always drove me to school so I didn't ride the bus that direction either.

The cool April air danced in my hair, I moved my right arm in the air outside the window. Beside me, Chace had begun to sing softly to the radio. Too afraid he would stop, I kept my face away from him. I assumed he didn't sing with his guitar playing due to an unpleasant voice. Very wrong. His voice didn't sound like one you would associate with country, which is what his music sounded like. His singing voice matched the one that spoke to me earlier. Calming, soft. In no way feminine, but never booming.

"I thought you didn't sing," I said to the passing air.

"This doesn't count." I heard a smile in his voice. The light one I loved.

"Why?" I turned to him.

"Singing to the radio doesn't count. Everyone does that." He reached over and lowered the volume.

"So?" I wanted to hear more. That voice, there was nothing like it. He was letting his guard down. From the moment I had met him, I had the pesky feeling that he was more reserved in my presence. These little glimpses of the guy I felt he truly was had emerged recently.

"So that would mean everyone is a singer," he countered, playfully.

"You know what I mean." I turned the volume up, just a little, testing.

"I just don't sing what I write. And it is very easy to sing along to someone else's voice."

"You have a nice voice." Did he sing for anyone at all? Maybe he sang on the deck, before I moved in.

"Thanks." He turned the radio off.

"Now you're not going to sing?"

"No, we're just almost there. We have to be quiet." His voice fell to a whisper and he lowered his head slightly; I mimicked his movements, like a shadow.

"Where?" The moon shone high in the sky, illuminating everything. I had no clue where we were.

"You haven't figured it out?"

"I never went down past the house. Where are we going? Are you going to tell me anything?" I started to take a good look at my surroundings. All I could see were trees and the glow of the lines on the road from our headlights. We pulled off the road to the right, before the bridge ahead of us, onto a worn down path, leading us below the overpass. Chace killed the lights and turned to me.

"You ready?" His excitement was electric. It felt tangible. I was afraid it would grab ahold of my arm and never let go. I wanted it to. I was afraid I would follow it, and him, anywhere.

This was not what I signed up for. A bitter spring creek? Snakes? Slime covered rocks? No. It was not warm enough to get in that running water. A summer float would be amazing, but it was definitely not summer. "I am not swimming in this cold ass creek at night."

"Good me either. C'mon." He exited the jeep and began walking back the way we entered, towards the main road. I cursed and flung my door open, scrambling after him. At the top, he crossed the highway to the road that would have lead us left. I caught up and saw his destination, freezing on the centerline.

"No, way man. No way. Nooooo way."

"What?" He turned and began walking backwards, grinning. He crooked a finger at me and beckoned.

"I'm not breaking into a church camp pool." I furiously shook my head to emphasize my point. I didn't move from the middle of the road. Luckily the pavement stretched out on both sides. No one would be popping around a corner to lay me out.

"It'll be okay." He turned again, walking forward once more.

"No way. I'm not doing it," I protested, yet I still followed him. It was true, I would follow him anywhere. Fuck.

"You can't just sit down in the jeep." He called over his shoulder, making his way down the hill, the pool sat at the bottom of it. I could see tiny little cabins surrounding the water. A large grassy area had two soccer goals and a large building was at the far edge of the field by the tree line.

"Why not?"

"Because I won't let you sit down there alone. We'll just have to leave. I really want to swim though. Please."

He had stopped and was giving me large exaggerated puppy eyes. I was sure they worked on everyone. They probably got him out of trouble time and time again. The moon made them glow eerily.

I turned to the right and saw my way out; I flung my arm out and pointed. "There's a house right there! Someone is going to see us!" He couldn't argue with that one.

"No, I know who lives there. They are out of town. See, no garage, no cars. It'll be fine. This isn't the first time I've done this. There's a spot where the chain link fence separates. It's easy to get in." I followed him, reassured by the fact that no one was home across the street. Once at our destination, Chace bent and began tugging on the chain link fencing.

"How many times have you done this?" I glanced back the way we came as he unwound wire holding two sections together.

"A dozen? I don't know, I've lost count," he shrugged. He knew I had given up.

"I'm surprised. I never would have pegged you for the trespassing type." I knelt down next to him, hiding from the road.

"It's been a really long time since I've done this. It was a common thing before I started college, the year I was acting like a huge ass hat."

"A huge ass hat?" I couldn't imagine him as anything but the saint he was. I was seeing a new side tonight.

"Yeah. Your mom's words. A big loser who drank a lot and didn't give a shit." He yanked his hand back and stuck his index finger in his mouth. "Fuck. Ouch."

"I can't imagine that. You're Mister Responsible."

"Yeah, Mister Responsible who got a C on his test today." His tone deflated. He went back to work on the very top of the opening.

"Hence the bad day?"

"Hence the bad day." Finished, he pushed the fence to the side and slipped in. Once inside he pulled it back for me to slip through. "So, I quit the bar. I should have given two weeks' notice, but I was so mad at myself that when I showed up for my shift I told Sheila it would be my last one. I felt bad after but I didn't know how to take it back. I could just hear your mom's voice telling me I need to focus on school more. So I did it. I'm glad I did. Just kind of pissed with myself."

"Tomorrow will be a better day." I walked around the pool, peering into the water. I couldn't tell how clean it was without the lights on at the bottom and on the sides. I hoped nothing was swimming around in there.

"Today has already improved." He walked the opposite direction.

"So, who did you come out here with during your brief irresponsible phase?" I imagined him skinny-dipping with pretty girls. He hadn't had a girlfriend since high school. I wondered if he played the field often. I wondered if he was more like me than I thought. I didn't know if I wanted to know the answer to that.

"Well, your brother would come out here with me. And, girls of course." I was right. I smiled to myself.

"Oooohh. Were they super impressed with your breaking and entering skills?"

"They were easily impressed," he answered, his tone matter of fact. "How was your day?"

"Crap, too. I've been sitting in that damn bed all day staring at a blank screen." The dull ache in my temple was nearly gone. The Ozark air was healing and my mind was thankful for the stimulation. For life, not the digital imitation of one.

"That bad?" He laughed.

"I'm dramatic, I know," I sighed.

"Do you always write at home?" He leaned up against the fence and laced his fingers into it above his head. I tried not to look at the sliver of skin that was exposed below the edge of his shirt.

"Not necessarily at home, but always in my room. I've rented a place north of New York where I can write. I can write in a hotel room. Always in bed. I hate sitting at a desk."

"So you do your job from bed. Rough."

"Shut up! It can suck." I stopped and stared full on at him from across the pool. I was beginning to feel nervous. I was alone in the dark with this beautiful man and despite resisting, I was beginning to desire him.

"So you aren't one of those authors who sit in a little coffee shop with her iced caramel latte writing all day?"

"No. I get distracted by the people and the noise. I need to be in a room, in bed, with music playing softly. No television. It's best if my iPad is across the room. Sure, I can surf the web right there on the computer but for some reason my iPhone and iPad tempt me more."

"Have you ever thought of trying something new? Maybe it will lift the block."

"Maybe." What could I try?

"When something stumps me I try to attack it from a new angle. That's what I want to teach children. To think outside the box and to step outside their comfort zone."

"I could try something new and still be in this spot. A big

fat boulder with no chance of moving."

"You act like you have something to lose."

"You're right," I surrendered. "I'll try it." I didn't know what exactly I would try. I had exhausted everything. I had flown all over the world.

"Tomorrow, then. I know exactly where to go." He pushed off the fence and edged towards the pool.

"Shouldn't I choose?"

"Nope. I know where we can go. I have the day off since I won't be at the bar anymore."

"I don't write around other people. I have to be alone. That's why I don't go to coffee shops. I guess that's why I live alone. Hey, maybe *you're* the problem." I pointed at him and faked angry eyes. "You should move out."

"No chance. I'm not taking you to Starbucks or anything. Give me more credit than that. Do you have hiking shoes?"

"So once again you're asking me about specific clothing I own and planning to take me to an unknown destination." I liked it. I liked this small trip here, more than any destination I had went to in years. I was seeing this small county that raised me with new eyes. This place that was nothing more than a synonym for too many ill words… Boring. Stale. Stifling. Wounding.

"Are you regretting coming here?" He broke me away from my thoughts.

"No." I felt calm for the first time in months, in this moment. He was safe. I had run from anyone who reminded me of those words for years, because safety was a lie. This did not mean I felt that he was dull, or ordinary. He had wildness in him. It was standing here with me now. His playful side. His childish side.

"Then shut it."

"Rude ass."

"Ass hat."

"Well, what are you going to swim in? You are swimming

right?" He bent his knee and reached down to one of his feet. He pushed off his worn converse and slipped his sock off, dipping a toe into the water, swirling it around. "It's a little chilly, but we'll warm up."

I had changed into a matching set of undergarments. Black. They didn't show much less than any of my bikinis did, but I was reluctant to undress. The moon was in full force. "Yes I am."

I slowly made my way to the small ladder. Chace's eyes left me as he turned his back and pulled his shirt over his neck with one hand. I found it hard to keep my eyes from his skin, it glowed in the light. It was unblemished, it begged to be touched. This was a horrible idea. Desire was burning inside of me, and it felt foreign.

I had lusted after many men, but this was new and left me feeling weakened and lightheaded. I turned and began undressing. I was overly conscious of my exposed skin. Lines of script were tattooed all over my surface. My arms, my back, my ribcage, my collarbone, my thighs. I loved words more than anything in the world, so I had branded the combinations closest to my heart all over my body. My left arm was covered in various pieces of art, a newly completed sleeve. I sensed his gaze on my back.

"I know you're thinking about it." His voice was low, I turned slowly.

"About what?" Suddenly I knew what he was referring to. I met his eyes, he had removed his glasses, and the blue was unreal in the light. He was open. I wanted to be as open as he was in that moment.

"My leg," he answered. "I didn't know if that's why you hadn't turned around. I figured you knew."

That was only partially true. The majority of my shock still stemmed from the warm feeling his words had been triggering in my stomach all evening. "I didn't. I mean, I did. I forgot." I looked down at my hands, clutching my top.

"I figured your mom or Andrew would have mentioned it."

"They did, a long time ago." I couldn't believe I had forgotten it. I was sick inside again, with the story. I tried not to look down at his leg. I didn't know what was worse. Staring at it or avoiding it. It did not bother me. It did not make him any less beautiful to me. And fuck, he was beautiful in that moment. His broad shoulders, his arms, everything. Everything was perfect. I wanted to make my way around the pool to him, I wanted to touch him. He was wearing nothing but a pair of boxers. He was exposed, but the air around him was closed. He was worried about the way I viewed him now.

"When did you lose it again?" I quickly sat down on the edge of the pool, lowering myself into the water, away from his gaze. I knew the story, I had just heard it again, but I wanted him to tell me.

Nine

April 1ˢᵗ

"I was eight," he began as he made his way to the steps on his end and descended. "My family and I went on vacation to Florida. Like every summer, my parents, my sister, Sasha, and me spent time with my dad's family at their beach house in New Smyrna.

Sasha and I would spend the days building sand castles and chasing seagulls. At night, my mom and dad would go out on the town while we stayed behind with my aunt and uncle, looking for tiny crabs on the beach. My mom loved to dance and drink, so my father would take her out to make her happy. Sometimes I would hear them fighting when they came back. My dad wanted the entire trip to be about family, but she wanted to have her own fun too."

His face and voice changed at that last sentence. Anger was woven in his brow. I lowered my jaw into the water so that only my nose and eyes remained above water. I remained silent, and he continued.

"My mom had my sister when she was sixteen, so I guess she felt like she missed out on a lot. Dad was twenty-two at the time and I doubt he ever had a wild streak. Family was what was important to him. I guess it was different for my mom. One af-

88

ternoon, my dad went fishing with his brother, and my mom left right after he did. Sasha and I stayed on the beach with Aunt Viv. A couple hours later, Mom came back and waved us up from the beach. She wanted to take us for ice cream. Once we got in the car, I could smell the alcohol."

He stopped speaking and I remained silent, letting him tell the story at his own pace. He dunked himself under the water and wiped his face. He kept his eyes from me, training them on the sky.

"I asked if we could wait until Dad got back but she said he wouldn't be back for a couple hours anyways. I felt weird being in the car, but she was my mom, so I didn't protest. I remember my sister reaching her hand behind her seat, looking for mine. I grabbed it. I didn't want ice cream anymore."

I felt sick at his words. I straightened my legs and rose halfway out of the water. I pulled my hair over my shoulder and started to wring the water from it. I wanted time to stand still. I didn't want to hear the rest. I knew how it ended. But he needed to tell me. He finally looked at me.

"We went over a bridge, but we never made it to the other side. My mom was smoking, something she never did. I assume it was a habit she only indulged in while drinking. We had the windows open and the air off even though it was sweltering. She dropped her cigarette and reached down to get it, her head was below the top of the wheel, she wasn't looking at all and her hands were away from the wheel. I remember my sister screaming and trying to steer from the passenger seat. It was too late by then. Our front bumper had hit another car and bounced us off, sending us fishtailing. I grabbed the seat in front of me and closed my eyes. We went into the bay. With our open windows, the car filled fast. My mom and sister had hit the dash and were unconscious. I tried to get Sasha. She was too heavy for me though. I barely made it to the surface. I didn't know my leg was broken then. I was in shock."

His voice trailed off, and I felt relieved. I didn't know if I could listen to anymore. The silence surrounded us.

"You didn't have to tell me all of that." My voice sounded small.

"It's public knowledge. Google me," he shrugged. His voice was light again. He wanted to move away from the story, from his story.

"I would feel bad for doing that."

"Why? I've Googled you before. Many times." His smile came back.

"Why?"

"I wanted to find anything you wrote. After that summer, everyone knew what happened to me. I couldn't take the staring. It made me feel worse. It made me feel broken. My dad couldn't look at me, so I hated being home. The teachers and my class-mates pitied me, so I hated being at school. My old friends didn't know how to act around me, so I spent most lunches sitting alone. Then one day your brother sat down next to me."

I smiled at the thought of my silly brother sitting next to a shy, quiet, Chace. He made everyone feel comfortable around him. He was so good at that.

"He was new. That was the year he started living with his dad and your mom. He didn't say anything, he just smiled at me and started to eat his lunch. It felt nice to sit next to someone and not worry about how bad they felt. You can feel that coming off people. He was just there to eat lunch. He came back the next day, and the next.

At the end of the week, he said I should come over to his house after school to hang out. It was the first thing he said to me, but it felt like we were already friends. We went to the old house with your mom, while she was working on packing up things in the attic, and ran all through the woods.

The next week I came over there three nights and we did the same. My dad didn't care if I wasn't home. He'd have more time to sit in his office and drink without having to be bothered with feeding me." He dunked his head under the water again and came back out, shaking his head like a dog, little droplets of water hit my face.

"School became bearable again," he continued. "I had your brother there. At nights, I had your family. I dreaded the weekends when I would be stuck at home with my father. I would waste my hours alone watching movies. He never cooked, but kept us stocked up on bread for PB&J sandwiches, and boxed mac and cheese. A lot of cereal was consumed. I began to view the time I spent home as visiting, and at your mother's was where I really belonged."

He felt like he belonged there. In that house. He escaped his nightmare in the place mine began. He had somewhere he could go. If only I had. I wrapped my arms around myself, a chill ran up my spine.

"Years ago, on one of the first cold fall nights, your mom insisted Andrew and I stay inside instead of roaming the woods," he started. "She had picked up pizzas that night to stop him from complaining about it. She was going to spend the evening painting the room I stay in now, your old room. Your stepfather was out of town on business. I remember we hung out in front of the fireplace.

Your mom pulled out a three ring binder. I knew she was a teacher so I figured she was going to give us some sort of assignment. Instead, it was a book. She said, "My daughter wrote it when she was in high school, it's never been published."

Your brother groaned and said he wanted to play a game. So, I took it. I read until it was time to go home, so your mom said I could take it with me. I went straight to my room when I got there and stayed up until one in the morning reading your story. I finished it. That was one of the first nights I didn't dream about my mother and my sister. I dreamt about the story you wrote instead."

I felt like I hadn't taken a single breath the entire time his light voice had hummed around that pool. It was swirling around me as I floated aimlessly in the water. My chest rose and fell erratically. My eyes were trained on the ghost of a shadow of my legs below the surface. I pulled them away and looked at his face. The belief that the eyes are the windows to the soul is well known. Everyone knows that damn saying, and for good reason. It is true. I felt like Chace's soul was staring back at me.

I had written countless stories when I was younger. I had no clue which one it could have been. I had forgotten nearly everything. Time will do that to you. A part of me wanted to forget them. In my life and in college, in everything after moving away from here, I had learned so much about writing. If I looked at those stories now, I would pick them apart, but my heart would be in them. That was the reason I didn't want to read them again. The stories I told back then would be better than anything I ever had published.

"What story was it?" I asked.

"The one about the man who played guitar by the sea," he replied.

"For the mermaid," I said. This obsession was brought forth by a certain red headed Disney princess.

"Yeah." He began circling around the back of me; I twirled in the water to continue facing him. "For the siren."

"I'm sorry," I whispered.

"Ah, life goes on. I get by pretty well. I play sports, I run, I swim. I don't let it get in the way. I've been without that leg for over half my life. I don't really remember what it's like to have the other one. And you're not the only one surprised here if that makes you feel better…"

We both knew I didn't mean his leg. He was obviously not held back by it, but I didn't press. It was his story, his tragedy. If he didn't want to talk about it anymore who was I to blame him? He had opened up to me. We had been doing that. Exposing scars, the way lovers do when their guards are let down and intimacy is inevitable.

"What are you surprised by?" I cocked my head to the side and my brow furrowed.

He pointed to my collarbone, to the lines inked along my skin. "You have a lot more tattoos than I would have guessed."

"I hear that a lot." After I've undressed, before sex, men always pointed them out. I blushed at the thought. Surely Chace could figure out when I heard that statement from men.

"Once the books took off, and I knew for sure that I could do this for the rest of my life, I couldn't stop myself," I explained. "I knew that I would never have to cover a tattoo for a job interview so I could get them anywhere. They're addicting. I would reward myself with them. I'd get one when I completed a project or when one of my books hit the bestsellers list. I'm running out of places though. I'll look like a walking book one day if I don't stop. One that doesn't makes sense." I laughed.

"How many do you have?"

"If you count my arm as one?" I looked up at the stars, they winked at me. Devils. "Twelve."

"Wow." He was still circling me, and I was still spinning.

I had the urge to walk out of the water, to let him look my body over, and count for himself. I silenced my forward thought. This was my roommate, not book research.

"You've never wanted to get a tattoo?" His skin was too perfect to mark. I loved all men. Tattooed, pierced, clean cut. I was not a woman with a type. Men were beautiful, and how they chose to paint their canvas was entirely up to them. I loved the art of them.

"Ah, not seriously. I mean, having a sleeve like that would be awesome, but I could never have one with my job."

A teacher with tattoos in a small Bible belt town such as this would be frowned upon. It was a town of gossip, judgment, and tight lipped fear. I could see his point.

"One of my best friends is working on her second sleeve. She's pretty bad ass." Gemma, my best friend in New York, was the one who went with me for my first tattoo, and every one thereafter.

"A sleeve on a woman is hot. I will not deny that." He smiled, his eyes crinkled slightly. The white of his teeth glowed.

"So, how many girls did you bring here?" I grinned back and arched a brow at him. Am I flirting? I could hear it in my tone of voice. There was a large switch inside of me; I knew when it had been flipped. I knew when every word coming from my mouth was a hook, a snare, a net. I knew when I was hunting. I had been fighting it. I had stamped the need down. It was out now. I needed to shove it back down. I shivered suddenly, and he noticed.

"You ready to go back?" He asked, avoiding my flirtation.

"Yeah, I'm turning a bit blue," I sighed. I swam to the side of the pool for the ladder. The two towels Chace had brought sat next to it. I climbed out and grabbed one, drying off quickly. I could hear Chace swimming over. He pulled himself from the water and grabbed the other and began toweling off too.

There's nothing like the rush of being near someone you find attractive. Knowing you want to touch them, but can't. I kept my back to him as I dried myself off. He walked past me towards the break in the chain link fence, his towel around his shoulders. I couldn't keep my eyes from his leg. It did not diminish my attraction to him. It did not deter me in any way. If anything, it made me want him more. All that he was, in spite of what happened to him, was beautiful.

The thought of losing Andrew ever, let alone at such a young age, despite our lack of blood relation, made my stomach knot. That kind of pain was foreign to me. All because of the selfishness of his own mother. A woman who wouldn't grown up. Her actions had ripped a family apart, sent two of them into the ground, and left two behind, broken. I was broken still. A death didn't shatter me, but I would take the death of the inno-cence I once owned over the death of someone I loved.

The drive home was quiet. Chace kept the radio off. I wrapped myself in a blanket he pulled from the back. My hair dried in the cool Ozark air. I felt alive. I felt happy. My anxiety had, once again, lessened in his presence. Maybe Kat was right. I was eventually, going to cave and act on this attraction. Maybe that was okay.

I was looking forward to the next day with him. I was feel-ing that high of spending time with someone who left you light-headed and warm. I had felt it before. I had used it as fuel and burned it off in pages. But I didn't want to do that with him. What would my family think if I burned him? Just like all the rest? I could just go back to New York. Shut them out again. But it was not something I wanted to do. I didn't want to be the girl holding the can of gasoline anymore.

We made it back to the house quickly. At the steps to the second floor, we hesitated to say 'good night.' I felt the lump in my stomach. The first date 'will-we-or-wont-we' lump. I could see a change in his ocean eyes as well. I darted up the steps be-fore I could make a fool of myself. I slept well.

April 2nd

For the second time since I had moved to Missouri, I found myself leaving the house with Chace, with no idea where I was going. I feared I was slipping into old reckless habits but Chace was not like any other guy I had ever pursued. Not that I was pursuing him.

I needed to remind myself of this. I needed to stamp down this attraction. I woke up feeling a little ashamed of my thoughts from the night before at the pool. I was familiar with 'next morning' shame, but I didn't drink last night. I didn't wake up in an unfamiliar bed. I didn't need to wash someone's sex off of my skin.

I always dated around my age and slightly older. Why did I find myself wanting this man? The obvious reasons flew to mind. He was beautiful. One could describe him as hot, sexy, cute, and, yes, he was all of those things. But I saw beauty. It was hard to listen to him speak, his soft voice sent me over the edge. He took care of his body, didn't take it for granted, and never let his leg hold him back.

His mind is what drew me to him fully. He could not sit idle, he devoured new information. Was this what I had been waiting for? Was this why I never let anyone in, and found excuses to cut every man out of my life?

This man was perfect in my eyes. I did not write men like him. I wrote sex crazed alpha males, and I hated that kind of man. But it sold well. I was a sellout. This boy, this man, I could want more with. The thought scared me. How could I know something like that? We were only beginning to get to know each other. It had to be lust. It was those blue eyes and that perfect smile. It was his hands. It was the way he looked at me in the pool. What would today bring?

I dressed warm. Spring was emerging more each day, but a bite was still in the air. I skipped makeup, threw my hair into a ponytail, and slipped on a ball cap. The house was empty when I made it downstairs. Chace was already outside loading his jeep. He was wearing shorts for the first time since I had met him. I guess insecurities tend to disappear once you strip down to boxers in front of someone. I blushed at the memory. Stop it, Sera. Stop it. He smiled at my approach.

He looked down at me. His height, suddenly more pronounced. "You ready to do this?"

I pretended to mull it over. "Sure. Although, I am still not sure what this little trip is about."

"Does it have to be about anything?" He countered. "Warm weather is coming. I have the day off. You have spent nearly all of your days inside. It's a crime." He swept his arm around and we both glanced at the tree line. Tiny buds of green were growing more each day.

"Ugh. You're a nature lover. I despise your kind."

"How could you live out here and not love it?" He raised his arms wider. He wasn't wrong. I loved it here, out in the open. But playing outdoors was something I had done little of since moving away, unless you counted long walks in Central Park. I shot him a smirk and hopped in the jeep. He replied with a grin and joined me.

We took off down the driveway, making small talk for the

forty-five minute drive to Camdenton Missouri. I ventured to this town during my high school years to shop at the mall in Osage Beach. It was a small town, known for its football team. I remember hearing about the castle there, but had never visited. Chace reminded me on the way there.

It, of course, wasn't a *real* castle. The structure was built in the early 1900's by a wealthy executive, who passed away before its completion, in one of the first automobile accidents. His sons finished the project in his honor. The castle acted as a hotel before it was destroyed by a fire in 1942. When we pulled up, I was immediately sad I had never seen it before. I had seen real castles in Ireland and Scotland, but there was something charming about this one. Perhaps because it was so close to my home. And the story behind it.

I hopped out as soon as we parked and started walking towards the trail leading to the structure. Chace called after me to wait. I turn to see him pulling a large box with a handle from his trunk and a blanket.

"Let's leave our phones here," he said. I walked back to him.

"Leave our phones? Why?" I didn't go anywhere without my phone. I was a slave to technology.

"No distractions." He shrugged shutting the back of his jeep.

"From what?"

"From that." He motioned to the castle. "From the outdoors."

"But what if we need help? What if one of us falls or something?" I clutched my iPhone in my hands, desperately.

He laughed. "Okay. I'll keep my phone. You leave yours here." He held out his hand to me, I stared at his palm.

"This sounds like the beginning of a missing persons case." I cocked an eyebrow at him. I was not scared of him. My senses were calm but I liked giving him a hard time. I strolled past him, over to the jeep and tossed my phone into the glove compartment. I turned to him and gave a 'happy now?' smile. He gave me an answer in his.

We headed up the trail to the castle. It didn't take long to meet the structure. It was beautiful in its ruin. I walked slowly, Chace trailing with his box. After twenty minutes of solo exploration, I found the spot where Chace had settled. He spread his blanket next to a ledge of the castle. His secret box was open and I saw what he had been lugging around. A typewriter. A beautiful black typewriter. One of my absolute favorite things in the world.

My mother had an obsession with them. Many antique models littered the home I was now living in. All were in astounding condition. This one I did not recognize.

"Where did that come from?" I asked as I took a seat next to him.

"It's your mothers. A recent find," he replied.

"I knew I didn't recognize it. I remember every one she bought. She had names for them." I ran fingers over the keys.

"I remember. I always wanted to play on them. Eventually she let me."

"She always was very protective of them. This one looks like, it's from the 1930s?" I had seen so many, and been on so many antique trips with her. I liked making a game out of guessing when they were created. I was nearly always right.

"Yep." Bingo.

"Wow. I love it," I gushed. "Why did you bring it up here?"

"For you to write on."

"What do you mean?" I turned to him. He was laying out on the blanket, propped on his elbows, his crossed legs next to the typer. His artificial one resting on top.

"You said you can't write. That you get distracted. Well you can't check Twitter on this. No Facebook. Nothing. It's just you and your words." He smiled shyly, proud of himself.

"True. But I can't imagine writing a novel on that." I was definitely born into the perfect era. I adored my Macbook.

"Just try it. You told me you moved across the country for writing. This isn't that crazy of an idea. What's the craziest thing you have done for writing?"

Basically prostituting myself was definitely the worst, but he knew that now and he still wanted to be around me. "I've done a lot of weird things. I myself was once in the bartending profession."

"Do tell." He sat up, leaning to one side on his arm.

I frowned. "For one month. I was horrible at it. I broke bottles and messed up drink orders. I assure you the character born from that experience was much more adept at it." I cringed at the memory. Worst month ever.

"What else?" He laughed.

"I bought a pickup truck with one of those tops over the bed of it, I threw a mattress back there and lived in it for three weeks in Montana."

"Just three weeks?"

"Yeah, that's all I could manage. When I was a kid, I didn't want to be a writer. I wanted to be an actress. I loved pretending to be someone else. I would perform little shows for my stuffed animals. My mom encouraged me to write down the stories I was acting out. I don't know how she knew I would excel at it. Maybe she didn't, maybe she just knew I would have been a horrible actress."

She was right. I couldn't hide my emotions from my face, and I couldn't fake ones that were not there. I was not talkative, I didn't need to be. It was always evident in my face.

"Okay, so using a typewriter doesn't seem all that crazy." He stood. "I'm going to walk around a little. I'll be close. Just shout if anyone tries to kidnap you."

I situated myself cross-legged on the blanket in front of the machine. I ran my fingers over the round black keys again. I hadn't used a typewriter since I was in high school. I wrote poetry on it. I loved the sound it made. I loved throwing the words out as they came. No backspace. No delete. It was all so real and permanent. I bled for that machine. I burned most of the pages.

My mother purchased a 1940's Royal for me. Ebony and beautiful. She said it matched me. I reached up and pulled my ball cap off, loosened my hair tie, and piled my dark strands into a knot. How did I ever forget the way it made me feel? I couldn't imagine using the one in front of me for anything else. But I had not written poetry in years. I did not know why I abandoned it. The idea of making money from it back then seemed ludicrous. Poetry seemed to be a forgotten art, and modern poetry was not as it used to be.

I had witnessed poets reach some fame after posting their work on Instagam. I browsed through a few of their accounts, but grew disgusted quickly. The most popular 'writers' wrote one-liners and clearly sought out 'Insta-fame.' They weren't writing honestly. Not the way I had as a child. I didn't click the follow button on any of the shallow, soulless accounts. They were easily identifiable. I did manage to find a handful of gems though.

I banished my thoughts of the digital world, actually glad my phone wasn't within reach, took a deep breath, and began to type. The words fell from my fingers. I should have known they would be about Chace. I didn't want them to be. I didn't want to repeat old habits. He wasn't like the others I had burned. I didn't want to make a dime off of anything that might come from this. Perhaps, that is why they fell so freely. He was walking poetry.

I hoped that he would not ask to read my work when he returned. I pounded the keys quickly. The typewriter was in immaculate condition, but still, old fashioned. It took time to get everything out. I tapped out poems, scattering them randomly across the single page, front and back. I ripped the paper out and folded it over many times, then slipped it into my pocket. I pulled out a fresh sheet from the back of the box and inserted it. I felt as if I had never stopped, that poetry had been spilling from my hands for years.

In that moment, I mourned those years. The years I did not use poetry to feel the kind of relief and release washing over me now. What would have come of those years? From the experiences of my twenties? It may have been wretched prose. It may have been perfection. I would never know. I didn't need to write to live. I was rich beyond my wildest dreams. No, I didn't need to write to pay my bills. I, still however, needed to write to survive.

I had been slipping further and further into depression with this writer's block. I could feel warmth creeping inside once again. I could kiss that kid. I could kiss him. Did he know this would happen? Could I show my fans this style of writing and have them accept it? The anxiety, it was still there.

I laid back down on the blanket, resting my right hand on the typewriter keys, closing my eyes, willing everything to be okay.

Chace found me like that later. A half hour later, a day later, who knows, it all felt the same. "Get anything done?" His voice broke into my daydreaming. He fell onto the blanket next to me.

"Yes," I sighed.

"Good," he replied. I waited for him to ask to see it. To ask about it. He didn't. "Want to put the typer away and hike some? It's so beautiful up here."

I sat up and lifted the typewriter out of its box. My mother always put their name there. I had been tapping away, with no introduction. I smiled at the name staring back at me. They fit. She was dark and beautiful and brutally honest. *Olivia.* I loved the name.

I stood and began gathering everything scattered around me. We trotted back to his vehicle, secured our items and found a trail. I followed him. He was more familiar with the area. I hadn't been on a hike in years. Many areas left me winded. Chace never seemed to break a sweat. We came upon a few anglers down by the edges of the lake, and a few people riding mountain bikes.

"Do you ride here?" I asked, as a couple went by us. It seemed so scary and dangerous. The steep hills caused me to slip numerous times in my boots.

"I have. It's fun and definitely challenging," he said over his shoulder.

"I'd like to try some time." I don't know why I said it. It terrified me. But trying new things seemed somewhat safer with him.

"Really?" He stopped and turned to me. I stopped and looked up into his eyes. "It's not easy. I'm not saying you couldn't do it. But it can be dangerous."

"I'd like to try some time," I repeated myself. "I've been looking at a few bikes online." He turned and began climbing again, holding a branch out of the way, letting me pass him.

"We can do that some time." We had made it to the top of a bluff. The lake below was beautiful. I held my hand over my eyes and smiled. The blue was clear from up here, which I knew was a lie. Down below you could see that the lake was fairly dirty. It was a party lake. Chace sat on a large rock and rested. I followed suit.

"I used to come here a lot. To think. And write. I would bring my guitar up here and just play a whole Saturday away. I'd scribble the music down in a notebook. Then bring it home and revise it over and over and over. I'm glad I'll have time now."

"Why didn't you go to school to be a music teacher?" It seemed like the perfect job for him.

"It crossed my mind," he admitted. "Sports and music, I love them both. Both can help children belong. The way the government has been killing the music programs in schools is a crime. It's just as important as anything else. I was just afraid if I got my degree for that I would have a harder time finding a position."

"Does Andrew have any gigs soon?" I reached down and began re-lacing my boots. The trip back down would surely be trickier.

"I'm not sure. I could find out. Would you like to go see him play?"

"Yeah, I definitely should. I'd like to see how good he is. See the thing he is passionate about. He always flew from one hobby to the next as a kid, never really settling on anything. But from what my mother says he really cares about this. I know his dad doesn't take it seriously, but if he is really good maybe I can help. I know some people in New York who may be able to help him out. He could fly back with me when I go home."

Chace's face twitched a little at my last few words. "When do you think you will leave?"

"I don't know yet. I did write some earlier. So maybe this place is helping finally." Maybe facing this place was helping. Maybe *he* was helping.

"Well, I hope it isn't soon. It's been nice not living alone."

"I agree."

Eleven

April 6th

The middle of the following week, I got a text from my best friend, Gemma, in New York. I hadn't been keeping in touch with her the way I should. I assumed the goings on of a small Ozark town would bore her. She was born and raised in the City.

> *Gemma: How's Missouri?*
> *Me: Good. Nice.*
> *Gemma: Any hotties down there?*
> *Me: That's not what I'm here for ma'am. Remember? WRITING!!*
> *Gemma: I know, I know, but what's the harm in having some fun too? But seriously, how is the writing going?*
> *Me: Horrible until yesterday... mostly I am distracting myself with other crap. I'm spending a lot of time with Kat, no complaints there. She is the other reason I am here.*
> *Gemma: How is she taking things?*
> *Me: Okay I guess. She is eating more, and settling in to her new place. Focusing on work, and I try to keep her distracted the best I can.*
> *Gemma: That's good. Have you heard from Tristan at all?*

Me: No? Why would I?

Gemma: Just curious if he has realized what a tool he is.

Me: Doesn't matter. And don't forget, I changed my number,

Gemma: I'm sure he could get the number if he really tried.

Me: I hope he doesn't.

Gemma: Wow. So you're serious about being over him huh?

Me: Ya.

Gemma: When you said you were moving away to the middle of nowhere I just figured it was because he broke your heart.

Me: I can see how it would look that way, but not the case.

Gemma: Who is the new guy?

Me: What?

Gemma: There has to be a new guy. Spill it.

Me: There isn't… …

Gemma: What's with all the '… … …' ???

Me: Super busy. GTG.

Gemma: I KNEW IT!!! Tell me now!

Me: Well I'm living with someone

Gemma: ARE YOU KIDDING ME!! WHAT!!

Me: Not like that. My mom kind of rents the house to one of my younger brother's friends. Gem, he is perfect. I couldn't write someone like him if I tried.

Gemma: How long have you been seeing him?

Me: I'm not. He just lives here. But seriously, I can't think straight sometimes when he is in the room with me.

Gemma: I need pictures. Send me a pic.

Me: Oh that's not creepy at all! 'Hey hold up a sec Chace, can I take your pic?' ??? NO!

Gemma: Facebook?

Me: Oh shit, yeah. Hang on a sec I'll go to his page and screenshot a photo.

I quickly found Chace's page and sent Gemma a photo. She began typing immediately.

Gemma: Son of a bitch...... You're life isn't fair. It's not fair at all! You get the best guys.

Me: I don't have him. Let's not get carried away. It will never be like that.

Gemma: Why not?

Me: He is 22. I'm beginning to believe my own mother thinks of him as a son. Plus, he lives here with me.

Gemma: You're bumming me out.

Me: I came here to learn how to write again. To quit acting like I'm a kid.

Gemma: I understand. But I want to visit soon

Me: No way. I know what you're thinking. I'll just come to you.

Gemma: I hate you.

Me: You adore me.

Gemma: True. Heading into the office. Ttyl. Hit that.

I laughed at her sign off. I quickly texted Kat to make sure we were still on for lunch. She had worked through lunch the past few days. Which was odd. I knew she was trying to keep her mind off things, but I felt something was more off than usual. She seemed distant in her texts. Not depressed, but just not her-self.

She texted back quickly. Confirming we would be eating. I dressed and got out of bed.

I wanted to go to the bike shop a few towns over. I wanted to be able to ride with Chace on the road and the trail at Ha Ha Tonka. After researching one afternoon, I decided on a hybrid bike that would be suitable for both. I was up for the challenge. I had always been a runner in New York. Never brave enough to cycle in the busy streets. I began running to get to the point where nothing on my body jiggled anymore as I went down the pavement. After I completed my goal I found that I couldn't go more than a couple days without hitting the pavement. I ran through the winter months as well.

When I ran, I let my mind run too. I would often draft scenes in my head, or stop to record them into my iPhone while my body was on autopilot waiting for traffic to cross and the walk signal to blink.

I was lost while I ran; my mind was everywhere contemplating my day, my relationships, work, and family. I hated going to the gym. The whirling of the machines, grunts of the men lifting weights, the babbling of women talking about their workweek. It was not relaxing to me at all. I tried listening to music in my headphones but the constant distractions took me out of my mind, out of my reflection.

My mother worried about my running in a busy city. I always ran in the morning, it felt the safest. I took the same route every time. I armed myself with my cell phone, a slim knife, and a bottle of pepper spray. If a man started to run behind me, I would stop to tie a shoe or check my phone, always facing him, and wait for him to pass. Maybe it was paranoia, but I certainly would not be ending up in someone's basement or dead in a ditch somewhere. Although I was cautious and aware, I didn't feel unsafe. Strangely, the crowds of people soothed me. I felt more unsure about running here, and thus had given up that love since coming home. The lack of physical activity only worsened my anxiety and depression.

I was looking forward to exercising with Chace. Though, my mind could already think of better ways to work up a sweat with him. Since that night in the pool, he had infected my mind. Amazingly, ever since the castle, I could write again. It had started early Monday morning. I awoke with a start at four in the morning, my sheets damp with sweat. It was not the first time inspiration hit at such an odd hour. I found that sometimes my best words came to me as I slept. If anything woke me, I had to get to my laptop as soon as possible before anything slipped away. What came to me filled me with unease, and a slight tingling sensation.

I had the most vivid sex dream about Chace. I immediately felt guilty. He took me out the day before to spark my imagination and here I was having perverted fantasies about him. Shit, damn, fuck. Old habits die hard.

I had pushed my guilt aside along with my covers and tip toed over to my computer, powering it on. I couldn't let it slip away. No matter how bad I felt. And why did I feel bad? I never wrote badly about a man I slept with. The men in my past who had been hurt knew before getting in bed with me that I wasn't looking for anything serious, if they developed attachments and the inevitable broken heart, it wasn't my fault. Not that I had any intention of getting in bed with Chace. He was too young, too nice. *Too living with me.* No no, that would never happen. But fuck, if it was anything like my dream, I'd be ruined for life.

I wrote for three hours about Chace. His eyes, his hands, his touch. I knew too much about it. I had been staring more than I wanted to admit.

I repeated this every night. Chace had more time on his hands, so he'd been playing below my balcony again. I would lie on the balcony above, a notebook in hand, my typewriter too loud to write as he played. It was the perfect tool for the writing I was doing. I was writing poetry again. I had felt three whole days of calm. I didn't care that it was not what my fans wanted. I knew this blind passion would not last. Eventually I would let it catch up to me, but for now I did not care. I was writing for myself and for Chace, my muse.

I fictionalized us in many ways. I was doing what I had done before, but without hurting someone. I was using my attraction for him, but it wouldn't wound him. As long as I kept our relationship platonic. I wanted to share my words with someone, that desire was there. I had never had that with the poetry I wrote as a teen, I would mostly write about things no one could know.

I was always adept at penning tales of unrequited love. Not many burn brighter. I was a masochist. I didn't have a style, it varied from piece to piece. I had found a small lock box in the back of my closet. I stored each piece there.

I decided I would tell Kat at lunch about my poetry. I met her at the deli across from her shop. They were a small family owned operation with the best turkey sub around. I remembered them from my teens. I had yet to find one to top theirs. We ordered what we used to as kids. Turkey, hot, with pickles on the side.

I dumped my news as soon as our waitress left. "I've been writing."

"What?!" My friend set her phone down and stared at me with her large amber eyes. "Really? That's great!"

"I know. I feel." I sighed. "Less heavy." I raked my hands down the sides of my face, letting them fall into my lap. I sat back and relaxed.

"What's the book about?" Kat asked.

"No book," I smiled. "I've been writing poetry."

"Really? Wow. I remember when you wrote back in school. You never would let anyone see it."

"I know. I know." Too many secrets lived there.

"Is that how you still are about it?"

"Actually, I brought some. I want you to read it." I pulled a few of the folded papers from my purse and handed them to her. She took them, and began reading. I felt a knot in my stomach immediately. Perhaps they were not as good as I thought. I wanted to get over my fear. I wanted to show someone what was inside of me. To feel a deeper release than the one I felt when the words left my fingertips. Kat smiled, and some of my fear subsided. She finished and handed the papers back to me.

"Who are they about?"

"Chace," I admitted. She smiled lightly, a knowing smile. I wanted her to know. I wanted to confess to her that I always had to have a muse. I had burned the rest, sure, but I needed them. She was my closest friend. She was the sister I never had. I wanted to confess. "I don't know what to do Kat. I can't get him out of my head." I groaned.

She arched on brow. "Is that a bad thing?"

"I think! Yes? I don't know. He's too good." The server brought out our subs and drinks. I took a bite of mine and moaned. It was so delicious. Kat started cutting hers up.

"What do you mean?" she asked.

I swallowed my bite. "He's kind. He's smart. He's stupid hot. Ugh." I picked up my sub and took another large bite. It was superficial. It was a crush. It needed to be fleeting.

"And these are reasons he sucks?"

"They're reasons *I* suck. Reasons I shouldn't go for the perfect guy." Deep down I knew he was too good for me. He was too good for a woman with a track record of using men.

"What do you mean?" Kat leaned both of her elbows on the table and stared at me.

I swallowed another bite. "I've never told you this. But everything I've ever written, is true. All of my books, I did those things. I can't write unless I have someone to write about."

"What's so wrong with that? Isn't that what most writers need? A muse?" She grabbed her Pepsi and slurped some down. She wasn't staring at me with judgment or shock. She was staring at me with her honest, open, Kat eyes. The ones that comforted me.

"Yeah," I managed, grabbing my own drink, suddenly parched. "But they don't hurt them all. I can't do that with Chace. I didn't just come back here to write. I came here to break the cycle."

"I think you're being too hard on yourself. I think, you've let this feeling, that you're doing something wrong, halt your writing. Maybe, that's why you haven't written in so long. You think you're doing something you shouldn't."

"But how am I not? I would go seek guys out, just to use them for writing." Maybe she didn't fully understand my confession.

"Sera," she placed her hands on the table, her voice was firm. "You are just going to have to put that behind you. Men use women all the time. Men use men. Women use women. Humans use humans. I know I'm the wrong damn person to talk to about this right now. You're just going to have to accept that I am on your side."

"I don't want to use Chace."

"That," she said, pointing to the folded papers by my phone, "feels different. I've read all of your books. They're hot. They're great. But this, this feels like, I don't know. It's not sex poetry. I mean, some of it is, but it's more. I'm not saying you love the guy. That's just stupid. But, if this is coming from him. Don't fight it."

"He mentioned that maybe you and I could go out with him and my brother this Saturday. I didn't commit to anything. Will you please go with me?" I pressed my hands together and pretended to beg.

She laughed and picked her sub back up. "Yes. I'd like that. Where are we going?"

I bit my lip. "Some honky tonk dance bar. Midnight Cowboy?" It was not my scene, and I doubted it would be hers.

"I've heard of it." She grabbed a few pickles and placed them on her sub, smiled, and took another bite.

"Thank you," I said as I took a bite of my own.

"No problem," she mumbled through hers.

"Not for saying you'll go," I clarified. "For supporting me. You always do."

She tilted her head and smiled, her warm Kat smile. "I always will."

April 9th

Saturday turned out to be one of the best days since my return to the Ozarks. Kat and I traveled two towns over to the closest mall. I needed a new outfit for that night. I needed to start drinking at noon. I needed a tranquilizer. Fuck. This was a ritual of mine. Going out? Buy new clothes. Chace was right. I had a problem.

My mother met us for lunch and drinks. After, we continued shopping to the point of exhaustion. I found myself nervous for the night's event. It was not a date, but I felt everything I used to feel before dates. The anxiety. The fear. The euphoric wondering.

I had seen Chace more throughout the week. He took me to pick up my new cycle. I sensed his awareness of a change in me. I was terrible at hiding these things.

Kat came home with me straight from our manic shopping and we ate a light dinner, spending most of the time getting ready. I promised to make up the couch for her if things got out of hand. She would probably benefit from a little reckless fun. She said she wanted to act more like me, after all.

I had not put on a pair of cowboy boots in years, but I purchased a new pair that day. I tucked them under dark slim boot cut jeans, and wore a billowy white top that fell off one shoulder. Kat curled my long dark locks, a task I hated and normally paid someone to do. In return, I took the time to straighten her wavy red strands. We were always trying to be who we were not, weren't we?

I pulled a bottle of wine from the fridge and popped the top, pouring each of us a glass. We sat on the porch and waited, and after a glass and a half, I heard Andrew pull up in his SUV.

I tipped back the last sip of my drink and we headed inside. I already felt a little light headed and wobbly from my drink as I walked through my room and gathered my things. I shut everything off and headed out, Kat rushed to my restroom, the wine hitting her. I took my time on each step downstairs; I would trip and fall easily in these clunky new boots, completely sober.

Even with this extra care, I felt my heel slip a bit on the last step when I reached the bottom floor. "Shit! Ugh!" I barked out as I grabbed the banister and dropped my keys. "Mother effer..." I sighed.

Reaching down, I heard a low chuckle behind me down the hall. The door to the laundry room was open. I snatched my keys up and made my way around the banister to face the person laughing at my misfortune. Chace was smiling at me as he folded laundry, shirtless. Fuck. Well that was hardly fair.

"You alright?" He smiled lightly, staring directly into my eyes. I felt my face heat immediately.

"Yeah, damn boots." I pointed down, as if he didn't know where my feet were. I looked up and saw him slowly take in my entire outfit, when his eyes finally made it back to mine I was thinking thoughts I shouldn't thanks to that glass of wine. He needed to get dressed. He needed more clothes on. Now. Andrew walked in the front door loudly, the way he did everything, pulling my eyes from his friend.

"Honey, I'm hooooooooommmmeeeee!!!" he sang. I laughed. "Jesus Chace, put a damn shirt on in front of my sister. What the hell is going on in this place while I'm away?"

I heard Chace laugh behind me and Kat laugh from the stairs. I rolled my eyes at my brother and walked over, slapping him on the arm.

He flinched dramatically. "But seriously man, put a shirt on and let's roll. These ladies can't be out late; they're getting up in the years." I slapped him harder. He flinched in earnest.

Andrew insisted Kat sit shotgun so that they could catch up. I was stuck in the back of the SUV with Chace for the hour-long drive, and it felt like I had been shoved into a dark room with him with no windows. For the entire drive he leaned forward and inserted himself into the conversation our friends were having. I didn't know if that was better or worse than him focusing his attention on me.

Kat's encouragement had me thinking something with Chace, something real, would be alright. That it wouldn't be the end of the world for everyone who knew us. I wanted to continue to write about him, regardless. This was a bad thing. I wasn't in New York anymore. I couldn't just use someone and discard them easily knowing the chance of running into them was slim. I was *living* with my new muse. I now considered him a friend as well. Each night my fingers hit the keys I pushed aside the guilt, reminding myself how much I needed this. To create a story, something more than my past work.

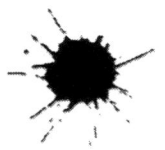

None of us had ever been to Cowboys before. It had only been open for about two months; the packed dance floor was filled with people still enjoying the newness of the bar. Despite being a so-called 'Western' bar, the company was mixed. Floating among the cowboy hat and boot wearing were those dressed in the trendy attire you would encounter downtown.

We strolled by the dance floor, a familiar old country song hit my ears as I took in the line of smiling people moving in sync to some sort of line dance. George Straight. I smiled. That was *real* country music.

We found four empty bar stools on the outside of the railing that bordered the dance floor, directly behind us was the largest of the three bars in the huge, open room. College-aged girls leaned over the bar, flirting with bartenders, sipping drinks, laughing. Andrew offered to get the first round and retreated with Chace.

"This feels awkward," Kat said, nudging me with her arm and directing her gaze at a girl, obviously the same age as the guys we were with. She was wearing very little clothing, shaking her hips on the dance floor. "Do we look like cougars?" She pointed her thumb towards the direction the boys went.

"I know," I groaned. "But let's not forget that you said this would be fun!" I raised my index fingers to my face and pulled my smile wide and stared at her creepily.

She playfully slammed the heel of her hand into her forehead, causing me to drop my hands and we both laughed. "I'm going to go check my makeup, be right back," she announced. Andrew and Chace returned with our drinks moments after.

My brother took a swig of his beer and planted his feet in

front of me, obstructing my view of the floor. I looked up at him. "Can I help you?"

"Kat is fucking hot," he declared.

I rolled my eyes and swirled my drink around with the straw. "Oh brother, noooooo…"

"What?" He shrugged his shoulders. Chace chuckled to my right, his shoulders bouncing up and down.

I narrowed my eyes at my sibling. "You can't say that about her." I took a long drink of my cranberry and vodka. It was strong.

"Why? It's true," he said, matter-of-factly.

"Okay," I said, setting my drink down and squaring my shoulders. "She is going through a divorce." I held up my index finger. *That's one.*

"I'm not saying I want to date her. I'm not saying I want to do anything with her. I'm just saying she is hot. It's just a casual observation." He held up his hands, one palm up, one with his beer, in defeat.

"Good, because you are too young for her." I held up my other finger. *That's two.*

"Well, that's not true," he said.

"She's too mature for you." I held up the third finger. *That's three.*

"Ouch." He clutched his chest dramatically. "And touché. I'm just having fun. I think she is too."

"I can tell she is. Thanks. I just wanted to get her out of that house so she could see that the world is still turning. I'd say we have been successful." Kat returned just as I finished talking. Chace moved from his spot next to me and offered his stool to her.

"Do you girls know how to do this?" Andrew asked, gesturing to the synchronized dancers. The foot stomping and hand clapping mesmerized me, and for a moment, I wished I had the nerve to dance. But I never did. I was the wallflower. I was the observer.

"No, never been to a place like this," Kat said, her mouth around her straw. "And Sera doesn't dance."

"You don't dance?" Andrew asked, incredulously. I was rewarded with this reaction every time myself or someone said it. Various outcomes came from this, some men immediately wrote me off as uptight. Some took it as a challenge, wanting to be the guy to get me out there. Some sat next to me the whole night, never leaving, knowing I had nowhere else to go.

"Nope," I answered, hoping the subject would change. Kat rescued me.

"Do you know how to do that?" Kat nodded her head to the dancers, and we all looked back at them again.

"Oh yeah, I had a girlfriend who loved line dancing. She taught me everything she knew."

"He is actually pretty good," Chace cut in. His voice was close. I looked up at him over my shoulder. He smiled.

"C'mon, let me show you." My brother motioned to Kat with his hand. Kat downed her drink quickly and followed him into the ocean of sweaty bodies. This couldn't be good.

"And then there were two," Chace laughed.

I huffed, my smile resembled a grimace more than anything. He walked behind me and took Kat's abandoned stool. It would be snatched if we didn't keep it occupied.

After watching our friends move awkwardly around the floor for two songs, in silence, Chace wandered off to the pool tables located near the entrance, leaving me to scowl alone. I placed my hand on the stool, daring anyone to steal it. No one attempted to ask me to dance; my resting bitch face scaring off any potential suitors.

I knew this couldn't last long, there was always one fool who sauntered up, swaying confidently, throwing out a lame line, *"It can't be that bad girl, let's dance, that'll put a smile on your face."* My response was always a tightlipped, "No, thanks."

I heard someone walk up behind me, I waited for them to pass me and head to the dance floor, but they didn't.

"She looks happy." It was Chace.

"Yeah, she does," I admitted. "It's nice to see her smile. She had gotten a little weird on me for a minute there, on her phone a lot. I was worried she was talking to her ex."

She hadn't been glued to her phone all night, but she had wandered off in a few stores earlier that day with her phone in her face. Something was up.

"The ex-husband?" Chace asked.

"Yeah, she kept texting. Every time I asked who it was she said her mom, or her sister, or so and so. I know she was lying. But she has done a 180 tonight."

"Well, that's good." A silence stretched between us. Tonight had been strange. Chace had turned shy again. I didn't know if it was the fact that we were with other people or not. It was the only thing to explain the difference in his attention. He turned to me. "So you really don't dance?"

"I don't really know any of those dances." Nearly everyone on the floor seemed to know what they were doing. I didn't know any country dances. They were swirling, twirling, smile machines.

"You can two-step," Chace stated.

"Is that a question?" I turned to face him.

"No. You can two-step. Anyone can two-step. Come on." He stood and walked around me. He reached for my hand and gently pulled it off the railing.

"No, I can't." I quickly pulled it out of his warm grasp.

"You can't always be the wallflower. Let's go."

He reached for my hand again, after a moment of hesitation I grabbed it and let him lead me to the floor. We stayed on the edge, away from the mass of bodies. He positioned us into the correct stance, pulling my left hand into his, grabbing my other hand placing it on my shoulder, and resting his other hand at the small of my back. I warmed at the feel of his hand against my bare skin there. My top sat a few inches above my jeans.

"Now, watch my feet," he instructed. His breath was on my ear; I fought the urge to look up into his eyes and trained my eyes down to our feet. I mimicked his movements, with my own boots.

We moved around the floor effortlessly. Every part of me was aware of him. I felt him in the places his skin touched mine, and the places I wanted him to. My pulse, beating in all the spots I craved his mouth, drowned out the music. Slowly I moved my body closer to his, his hand dug a little into the small of my back, and I sighed slightly in his ear. Involuntarily. Fuck.

His own mouth, so close to my ear, set me on fire. His soft voice swept through me. "You say I'm easy to talk to, well you are too. But I hold myself back sometimes."

I caught Kat's wide eyes over the side of Chace's arm. I turned my face, and tilted my head up towards his ear. "Why?"

"I'm an outgoing guy, despite everything in my life. I can talk to anyone, I make friends easily. But I don't do serious talks. Not with many people. I mean, a lot of guys keep feelings in, so I guess it's not entirely abnormal."

"I guess." Society pushed men to believe they had to be stoic. I disagreed. I was attracted to artists, and creative minds. They tended to be more open. If they had trouble voicing their feelings, it came out in their music, their work, their books. Often I was the taciturn one in the relationship.

Chace pulled back, and looked down at me. His gaze was penetrating. "I like you," he said, simply. We both knew there was nothing simple about those words.

I stared back. We had stopped dancing. Couples zipped passed us, most likely shooting daggers at us. I didn't care. "I like you, too."

"More than a friend," he stated. His tone was confident. His eyes were not.

"Me too." I felt something release inside of me. I had said it. Not to myself, not to Kat. To him. Everything would change.

"Okay," he replied. It was all I needed. He pulled me close again. We danced for one more song, and then made our way back to Andrew and Kat, where they wore knowing looks.

April 9th

The drive to the bar was hell, but the drive home burned hotter. It felt as though Chace was all around me. Chace, having only drank water or soda all night, was the DD. I was drunk on vodka and his touch.

Andrew jumped in the back as soon as we reached the parking lot. Kat followed him closely. Too closely. They were both quite drunk. They rambled loudly in the back seat, demanding we turn the volume up when we reached a song either of them liked. They sang loudly and carried on about a couple that had been bumping into them while they were dancing.

I wasn't worried about my friend falling into something reckless with my brother. Although she was tipsy now, she always did the mature thing. She was the anti-Sera.

Chace and I were completely silent. Nothing we wanted to say could be said in front of the two jabber jaws in the back seat. Not that they would remember it. The hour dragged on. I stared out the window, too afraid to turn my face. Chace's scent filled the vehicle. It wasn't overwhelming, but it was all I could focus on. It was clean and male. Thankfully, the bar was smoke free.

An old 90's country song came on the radio that I recognized, I turned away from the window and reached for the volume. Chace caught my eye.

"I love this song," I murmured.

"I do, too," he replied. I turned back to the window. When the chorus started, I heard Chace begin to sing along. I smiled lightly and sang softly to myself as well. Maybe I didn't want to make it home. Maybe I wanted to sit here in this seat and listen to him sing for the rest of my life. Time sped up, as it always does when you experience a perfect moment.

I was having more and more of those perfect moments with him. The closest I had ever been to a serious relationship was with Tristan. Yet, in the short time I had known Chace I felt more drawn to him than my ex. I didn't know his favorite color. I didn't know how he liked this steak. I didn't know his favorite sports teams, but I knew him. And he knew more about me than many who had been in my life for years. All of this happened without our lips touching. I was lost. Chace sang to nearly every song for the rest of the ride.

As soon as we parked in front of the house, I propelled myself from the vehicle. I felt fuzzy from my drinks, and Chace's voice.

I made it inside quickly and busied myself in the living room and the downstairs bath, setting it up for Kat. I pulled out a brand new toothbrush from under the sink and laid a fresh towel on the rim of the claw foot tub.

In the living room, I pulled out an extra blanket from the large antique trunk sitting under the front window, and placed it at the foot of the couch. Satisfied, I exited the room to find Chace pulling blankets from the hall closet for the leather couch in the office. I walked over to the room and peeked in to find Andrew, already face down. I looked up at Chace and he shrugged, then we both laughed.

"Where's she at?" I asked in a whisper. It was unnecessary. My brother would not be waking. He motioned toward the kitchen. I walked past him into the room. Kat was tossing a pill, probably an Advil, down her throat and chasing it with a large glass of water. Smart girl.

"I set up the couch in the living room," I began. "It's very comfortable. I napped there last week."

I reached for the cabinet door and got a glass down. I spotted the Advil container on the counter and grabbed it. I popped out a few and threw them down my throat, then chased them with a large gulp of tap water.

"Thanks," she groaned. She took a seat at the bar and smiled. "Tonight was fun. I haven't laughed that much in a long time. Your brother is still hilarious."

"Yeah, he always was a clown, huh?" I gripped the counter behind me and hoisted myself up onto it. Andrew was the guy who could make everyone laugh. I always figured it came from his mother, because his father had a very wooden sense of humor.

"Yeah, I remember," she agreed. "He was always cracking jokes and trying to get our attention. But we were mature teenagers and thought his jokes were silly back then."

"Oh yeah," I reminisced. "Very mature teenage girls." We both laughed.

"Well I'm going to crash," Kat said through a stretch. "Be good."

She raised her eyebrows at me and walked out of the kitchen. I didn't reply. I hoped Chace was already in his room. I couldn't handle seeing him anymore that night. The liquor was coursing through my veins. I had been able to keep the 'old me' at bay for a while, but now she was close to breaking free.

Once I heard Kat close the French door that closed off the large living room, I rushed to my room. I didn't make it far.

"Where are you going?" Chace sat at the top of the steps. In my way. His arms rested on his knees, hands crossed at the wrist in front of him.

"Bed." I pointed at the door on his left.

"Why are you going to bed?" His shy smile was back. I stared down at my feet.

"Would you prefer a lame excuse or the truth?" I looked back up.

"Dealer's choice." He stood.

"I don't want you to touch me anymore." It was a truth. A half-truth. If he didn't touch me, I could go to sleep and wake up a good girl again. Not the girl I was in New York. I could resist him from the quiet of my room. I could resist him if he was out of sight. I could sit up there and write about all the things I wanted him to do to me in this moment. That was harmless. This, here now, was not.

"'Lame excuse' it is. Nice." He laughed rising and making his way down the steps towards me. I backed up towards the kitchen, missing the doorway, hitting the wall in the small hall. He rounded the banister and walked to me. He stood in front of me, closer than arm's length, and reached out tentatively, brushing the hair off my bare shoulder.

"You really need to quit that." I took a breath.

"You don't like me touching you?" He moved closer, his fingertip slowly trailing down my arm, tracing the lines of script there.

"Irrelevant," I swallowed. "You're too young for me to be-ing doing this."

"Well at least we are past denial now." He let his hand fall to his side and stared into my eyes full on. I wanted to turn away. I needed to. We stayed like that for what felt like forever, until I was able to gain control.

"This is a horrible idea." I turned my head, avoiding his gaze. My hair fell to the side, exposing my neck to him, an invitation. He moved closer. I wanted him to taste me, but I only felt his breath there. He wouldn't touch me until I told him what he needed to hear.

"Tell me 'goodnight,'" he whispered. He brushed the hair

from my face and lowered his mouth to my ear. "And I'm gone."
I was frozen, no sound came from my lips. His opposite hand
settled on my hip, his thumb dipping under my top.

"Do you care about my age right now, Sera?"

His question caused me to whimper as I gripped the wall
behind me. He had barely touched me and I felt like I might lose
it at any minute, what would I do when he kissed me? He knew
where my thoughts were.

"Do you want me to kiss you, Sera?" Fuck. Another inco-
herent noise escaped my lips.

"Yes," I managed. My voice was breathless. Every nerve in
my body was at attention, waiting for him. He was everywhere
all at once, his legs pressed against mine and I parted them to let
him enter the space, his right hand moved to my face, his fingers
lightly swept the curtain of hair from my face. His left hand cir-
cled my wrist and slowly drew my arm behind me.

I turned to him, making eye contact again. His eyes were
dark pools of inky blue. I reached up grabbing his shirt and making a fist, I didn't want gentle.

He moaned, pressing his forehead to mine. Both hands
grabbing my ass, he lifted me up and my legs instinctively
wrapped around him. I pressed into him, and another noise escaped his lips. I just wanted them on mine. Why wasn't he kissing me?

As if sensing my thoughts, he answered. He was so close
his breath flowed into me. This had escalated so quickly. I was in
familiar territory. This was where I was comfortable. Lust, se-
duction, need.

And yet, I felt off kilter. With him everything was different.
My heart was in it. And that scared me.

"I want to kiss you right now, Sera, but I don't want you to
be drunk. I want you to remember it tomorrow." His voice was
low and close.

My stomach flipped; did he really just say that? Immediately I felt my face heat up, I pulled away, despite his words, the need, I felt rejected. Chace was one of those people who always maintained eye contact, it unnerved me, and right now, it was turning me to mush, burning into my core like a laser. I stared at my hand gripping his shirt. I started to release my grip, my breathing had picked up as well. I knew he was taking this all in.

"Chace, you're too young for me..." I immediately regretted the words. It was the second time I had said them, but after his touch burning into me the way we both knew it had, I felt wrong for saying them, it was dismissive and felt condescending. He was the most mature guy in his early twenties that I had ever met, certainly miles past the ones I dated when I was his age. I peeked up at him and was met with a sly smile. I hadn't wounded him.

"That is why I can't kiss you. You're tipsy. You keep repeating yourself." He set me back down on the ground. My boots made a loud sound on the wooden floor. I grimaced, remembering my brother was so close, around the corner. If he was awake everything would have made it to his ears. I heard a snore and let out a relieved breath.

I felt like I was on fire, every nerve in my body was waiting for his touch to return. God, I wanted this, didn't I? How had this happened? Seven years separated us but the only distance I could see was what was now between us, I moved my arms to the side of my body and gripped the wall behind me.

He walked past me into the kitchen. "I know you really don't care about my age." He tossed the comment out. I grabbed onto it.

"It just doesn't seem smart," I followed, smoothing out my ruffled clothing.

"You always weigh the pros and cons before you kiss someone?" He had me there. He grabbed the bar stool closest to him and sat on it, facing me.

No, I wasn't fighting this because of his age.

He wore dark denim over scuffed boots, and a fitted heather grey t-shirt. A loose plaid shirt hung on his shoulders. His light brown hair was freshly cut, and a light stubble covered his jaw. His full lips were inviting, begging to be kissed, crimson and raw. Jesus, I wanted him.

He was living with me though, and one could argue that this would be monumentally stupid. Kat would disagree, she was now pro-Chace.

"No, I don't," I finally responded.

He sat up and walked back to me. He reached out and took one of my hands, again, sending electricity throughout me. I could feel the heat from his body and his voice was low and close to my ear.

"Okay," he said, pulling the tender side of my wrist to his lips. He placed a light kiss there. Then he was gone, walking slowly past me towards the door to the kitchen. He turned and backed into the doorway, raising his hands above his head, gripping the frame, the smirk was still there, taunting me. "I'm going to bed. I think I am going to get up early tomorrow morning."

The change of subject was unexpected, and slightly disappointing. I liked the game, the feeling of being pursued, I think most women did. We craved feeling desired, it made giving in so much more rewarding.

I didn't often pursue. I wasn't conceited, I did not think I was a 'ten,' but I knew how to play my strengths, knew how to lure them in. I needed to feel wanted, it gave me power, and it made me feel worthy. I craved the approval, to hell with any respect I lost to gain it. I sure was a classy broad.

When had I become that girl? Had I been doing that with him subconsciously? I let out a heavy breath and reached behind myself, gathering all of my hair and pulling it over my shoulder. I saw his gaze flicker to the opposite one, the one exposed by my falling shirt. The one that his mouth had been so close to earlier, and then his eyes landed back upon my face.

I was toying with him now, it was ingrained in me, he had laid his desire out for me to see and now I had to pull him in.

"Okay," I said.

This would not affect our friendship. We could go back to normal after this confession; I wouldn't feel the need to ride this train after the alcohol had been rinsed clean of my system. Chace winked at me and turned to go, I followed and looked around the corner as he made his way to bed. He stopped a couple steps into his room, his last words curling over his shoulders.

"I am going to kiss you, Sera, and you're going to want me to."

Well, shit.

April 10th

The next morning brought spring rain. I woke at seven to the pitter-patter sound on the rooftop. It was soothing, and nearly lulled me back to sleep, until I remembered the previous night. I remembered Chace's hands on me, his breath so close. There was no way I could go back to sleep.

I wondered how it would be between us now. I heard the sound of dishes and voices from the floor below. The man was inhuman. To me, rain on Sunday morning meant one thing: sleep in until noon, get up, eat some food, read a good book, take a nap, eat some dinner, and then settle in for a movie.

All of those things sounded divine. I wondered what Chace did on rainy days. Would he survive a day where he was cooped up inside with nothing to do? He didn't appear to have an idle gear.

I groaned into my pillow and rolled myself off the bed and headed to the bathroom. After rubbing some moisturizer on my face and brushing my teeth, I slipped on my robe and some slippers. The hardwood floors stung my toes, the rain had brought back cooler temperatures and they were seeping into the house. I opened my door and was greeted by the scent of bacon.

I found Chace and Andrew in the kitchen talking, with Artax at their feet waiting for scraps. "Morning," my roommate called over his shoulder.

"Morning," I sighed. I took a seat next to my brother at the bar. He smiled a greeting. I smiled back.

"It's supposed to rain all day," Chace reported. "I know we talked about riding, but it looks like that won't be in the cards." He pushed eggs onto three plates sitting on the island.

"Darn," I said.

"I can tell you're heartbroken," Chace said over his shoulder as he reached for another pan on the stove.

"How in the world are you guys up right now? I mean. I know how you are Chace, but bro, you were plastered." I nudged him. He had placed his face into his hands. He nearly fell out of his stool. I wasn't that strong.

"I have band practice at noon and I can't sleep in if I'm not in my own bed. Stop talking so loud." He groaned.

I ignored him. I wasn't talking loudly. "Do people ever come to those? I still haven't heard you play."

"Yeah, sometimes. You could come with Chace when he brings new lyrics." He lifted his head from his hands and pointed at Chace's back. "Man, you owe me some."

"I'll probably write some today. What are you going to do today, Sera?" He walked to the fridge and pulled out O.J., then retrieved three glasses from the cabinet.

"Attempt to write, too?" My brain wasn't up for writing at the moment. But maybe after a nap.

He handed me my glass. "I have a long list of spring cleaning chores to do. I've been trying to knock a few off the list each week."

"I can help with that if you want," I offered. It was the least I could do. He had made this delicious breakfast for two useless zombies.

"No, you don't have to. Doing those chores is my rent. And now I have the time."

"Again, I own the house, remember? I can help." I stuck my fork into a piece of sausage on my plate. I needed food.

Chace began eating, standing at the island. "I don't mind. It's okay."

I pointed my fork at him. "You can either tell me something on the list, or I'll just randomly clean something. Your choice." I shrugged my shoulders and aimed my fork at my hash browns.

"Okay, but only one thing on the list." He smiled at me. There was something in his eyes. I hoped Andrew couldn't see it. "Maybe instead of cleaning you can just help me give Artax a bath?"

"Is that a two person job? Aiden gave him one that one night."

"Yes. He hates baths." He stared down at the dog at his feet. "Yeah, you." He looked back at me. "Just not when Aiden does it for some reason. It's a huge pain in the ass to give him one. And he is starting to smell. He doesn't really understand that if it's raining he should probably come sit on the porch, not hang out in the yard and get drenched."

"Yeah, I can smell wet dog right now." I scrunched up my nose.

"I thought that was you, Sis." Andrew elbowed me. Laughing at his own joke. He was always doing that. He didn't need anyone else to laugh, he cracked himself up.

"Funny," I said through a mouth full of eggs and bacon. "Where's Kat?" I had completely forgotten about my friend. Andrew laughed again, beside me.

"She left right before you came down," Andrew began. "Don't worry, I walked to her to her car and gave her a big smooch for you."

I choked on my mouthful of food. My brother pounded on my back, and I swallowed. I took a sip of my drink and glared at my sibling

"You are kidding, right? Please tell me you are kidding," I

pleaded. My eyes had to be the size of our plates.

Andrew smirked. "Yes, I am kidding. Calm down. Jeez. But no seriously, she left a little while ago." He scraped the last bit of his breakfast into his mouth and set his plate down. Burping, he patted his belly and grinned at us. "I better get going too." He took his plate to the sink and waved at us as he left the room.

The rest of the meal was rather quiet, with no buffer around. Eventually, Chace asked me how I felt and I told him I was fine. I asked him how he felt and felt silly immediately since he had not drank any alcohol. Eventually we just ate in silence. When I was done, I rinsed my plate and left the kitchen. I felt as though Chace's eyes were on me the entire time.

I retreated to my room, away from the tension, and tended to social media. I set up ten giveaways for my trilogy on Twitter, Facebook, and Instagram. I arranged for the books to be sent to Missouri so that I could autograph them as well. I always did giveaways around the release of my next novella, since I had nothing for my fans maybe this would harbor some good will and patience.

After that task was completed, I opened my balcony door and plopped onto my bed to think. The rain outside caressed my ears and nearly lulled me back to sleep. The dusty room was cozy, and my down comforter surrounded me. Back in New York, I often played storm sounds through a small speaker attached to my iPhone at night, but nothing compared to the melody playing on the green tin roof above me now.

On stormy writing days in New York, I always found myself weaving the rain into the story, as if it had infected my soul, and then slowly dripped through my fingertips. The scent of the moist grass slowly filled my room, an aroma I had missed in the City.

As a child, I loved and hated rainy days on this land. I would wake with a sense of adventure, having already planned the night before where I would escape to the next day, only to wake to rain. We always occupied ourselves with fun and meaningful activities indoors but I would pout at my ruined plans and the suffocation I felt.

On one particular Saturday in spring, I snuck out into the rain. I thought it would be fun to climb up the barn and play in the downpour atop the metal roof. I was able to enjoy my fun for nearly ten minutes before my mother caught on. I'll never forget how mad she was at me. She scolded me about how I could have been struck by lightning. I retreated to my room, head towards the ground, and remained there for the rest of the day. I was grounded from the fun plans my mother had made for the four of us. She brought me my favorite lunch, peanut butter and jelly, extra jelly, though. Therefore, I knew she still loved me.

I wrote a story that day. I was in my phase of being fascinated with the Greek and Roman gods. But I wanted to make up my own god. So I created a story about one of Zeus's sons. He, of course, had many, but I wanted to create one entirely of my own. He had many of the same elemental powers as his father, but shared none of the promiscuity. He loved one human woman, often watching from his home in the sky. She knew he was there, waiting for her to commit to life with a god. She would stare up at the sky for long hours, communicating silently with him.

Then, one rainy night, she climbed the tallest building in the City during a violent storm. She wanted him to finally take her, to take her away from the monotony of day-to-day life without him. She longed for more. But Zeus's son hesitated. He worried he would ruin her life, taking her away from all of her friends and family.

It pained him that she had been distancing herself from them for months, preparing for this day. His love would be nothing more than a selfish cruel thing if he took her. It would benefit only him. He stared at her tear stained face as she knelt on that rooftop, crying out, wondering where he was. Why would he abandon her? Had she imagined him creeping into her dreams?

He wanted her to have a child, to love a man who could be there for her day in and day out in her human world. That man was not him. He could not be his father, Zeus, taking what and who ever he wanted on a whim. He resented him for the lonely life he gave his mother. After impregnating her, he left to raise a son that never fit in. He tried to make it up to him, bringing him into the sky after the death of his mother, to live with the gods.

I wrote poetry again that morning. The previous night fueled me. I typed furiously at my vanity on the typewriter. Everything seemed normal at breakfast, but there was a charge. I hoped Andrew didn't notice.

After another hour of writing, I changed clothes and headed down to brave the tension. I found Chace in the kitchen mopping. A long list of cleaning chores sat on the counter. Without saying anything, I picked a chore and set out to do it. We continued like that for the next two hours; wordlessly walking by one another. When he saw my finger grazing "mop living room" he retreated to bring me the mop. I thanked him with a small smile. I didn't know what we would say when the chores were done. I wondered what was being said now in our silence.

He walked by me once, a bottle of Windex in his hand, the other slightly grazed my arm. A burn was left behind. I kept my eyes on the ground, my face a deep crimson. When I finished my last task, I headed to the kitchen and found Chace crossing out his last chore.

Was I foolish to believe this would not have happened? Two young, available people, with a mutual attraction, living under one roof. There were no real obstacles in the way of hook-ing up.

Finally he spoke. "Do you want to watch some T.V.? I'm not ready to write."

I nodded, not yet able to speak. I followed him to the living room and took a seat on the opposite side of the couch. Every sound felt so loud. The hush of his breathing, the rain on the roof, the sound of the television powering on.

I heard his final words from the night before over and over. I tried to silence them as he turned something on. He began flipping through the DVR recordings. He landed on Friday's Tonight Show episode.

"Good choice," I said.

"I love Jimmy Fallon. He just seems like he would be a nice guy."

"He is." I baited him, relieved we would have something interesting to talk about and hopefully break the tension.

He turned to me, not yet pressing play. "What do you mean 'he is'? You've met him?"

I shrugged. "Yeah. I was on his show."

"No way!" Chace set the remote on the coffee table and swung his leg onto the couch, facing me full on.

I laughed. "Way."

Chace shook his head; I glanced at him and smiled. "I've seen every one of his Tonight Show episodes. I would have remembered you."

I settled back into the couch, reached for the throw blanket, and wrapped it around me. "Well I was on his Late Night show. It was right when the first movie adaptation of my books was releasing."

"You have no idea how jealous I am right now."

"You must not be that huge of a fan if you didn't see all of his shows," I teased.

"That must have been before I got a DVR. I work late, and when I don't, I just pass out."

"Well I'm sorry you missed it." I glanced at him again, and then back to the silent television.

"Did he have you play a game with him?" He asked.

"Yes," I blushed.

"What was it?" His voice told me he noticed my skin turning.

I sighed. "Well, he had the Roots read dialog from the first book. Some of the steamy scenes, and they did it very comically. I had to keep a straight face during it!" I laughed loudly at the memory. "Oh, I failed miserably. It was so funny."

Chace laughed and punched his leg playfully. "I'm going to have to look that up."

I pointed to his phone on the coffee table "It may be on YouTube. His show was by far the most fun I had promoting the film. I'd love to go on his new show."

"There's one more movie coming out, right?"

My laughter left me. I shuddered at the reminder that I had to promote again, alongside Tristan. I had to smile, laugh, and pretend. "Yeah."

"Well, maybe you'll get to."

"Yeah maybe, they go for the stars of the movies and the directors before the author. I got lucky with that last one."

"You never know. I hope you get to go back on."

"Me too," I offered.

My thoughts suddenly turned dark. I didn't want to have Tristan, and our drama on my mind, but it was there. I had been living in a nice little bubble. A place where reporters, agents, and publishing companies didn't exist

That life was not gone; it was waiting for me, like a scorned lover. It would be back once this tryst was over. I looked over at Chace, he had started the episode, and was smiling at the television.

He wasn't some simple affair or some simple distraction. He was more. We had fought it last night, but I knew temptation was not gone. It would be back for us. It would rush back with a simple brush of fingers, a lingering look. He was the only lover I was concerned with. My past could wait a little longer.

April 10th

After a couple hours of television, Chace said he needed to start writing. I agreed and headed up to my room to type. Before long, I heard him on the balcony below, strumming his guitar, so I decided to join him. I grabbed a pad and a pen, not wanting to distract him with the loud noises of my typewriter. Chace stopped playing for a second as I joined him in the chair across from him.

He began again when I opened my notepad. We continued our silent conversation from the couch. I felt him glance at me as I wrote; when I looked up, he was looking down at his guitar. It felt like we were dancing again.

When he paused to write in his own notepad, I paused too. I listened to the scratching of his pen. I wondered what his lyrics said. I longed to go to one of Andrew's shows. I needed to hear the words coming from the man before me. I didn't want to deny my feelings anymore. I didn't want to stay away. I couldn't if I tried. If that was the only option, I would have to move back to New York.

I couldn't continue to live in this house with him, feeling the tension day to day. It was more dominant than the demons living there. The consequences may eventually outweigh the passion I knew we had. I wondered what my mother would say. I had done plenty of things my mother would not approve of. Far from here, where she could not see it all play out. Surely, she will frown upon this. This man before me was as close to her as her own stepson. I was always going to be a selfish girl. I was always taking lovers, and running from consequences.

Fact: Chace was too good for me. I looked up to see him staring at me. His blue eyes were light in the gray light of the rainy day.

"What?" I whispered.

"You stopped writing." He pointed to the pen dangling between my fingers.

"Yeah. Just thinking." I set the pen down and stretched out on the reclining chair.

"How has the writing been going? I hear the typewriter upstairs a lot." He relaxed too, putting his notebook to the side.

"I've been writing a lot actually. It's crazy. I don't know if I will be able to do anything with it. But I guess I'll worry about that later." I shrugged. I had been thinking more and more about organizing all of the poems. Maybe a book would come of it. Maybe not.

"What changed?" He asked, turning his head to the side.

I couldn't give him the truth. *You changed everything. You made me a poet again. No, not again. You reminded me that I am a poet.*

"I don't know," I lied.

Chace laid his guitar to the side, perhaps pondering my answer. I wondered when we would discuss the night before. If we ever would. It was generally a "woman thing" to want to over talk every situation. Over analyze every situation. Dissect every situation. It was one of my traits.

It was my job, too. I would share a night with a man only to tear apart every bit of it the next day on a page. I always carried a notebook with me in my purse. They had been empty for too long. I felt sick at the thought of my past. I was a parasite. He had to know I was writing because of him. That I had written all morning about the night before. He was a smart guy. I could bullshit any man, but I felt Chace was immune to me. Honestly, I had no desire to bullshit him in the long run.

Still, I just couldn't bring myself to confess. I saw Chace stand from the corner of my eye. "Go put your rain boots on," he instructed. "Grab an umbrella or a jacket. I want to show you something. Bring your notebook."

Once ready, he walked outside and I followed. He grabbed my hand, and started to run across the lawn, towards the woods. I knew where we were going. I smiled at the thought, at the feel of his hand in mine.

Our destination was not far into the woods. My rain boots were stiff and hard to run in. Chace didn't run quickly, so that I could keep up. We reached my old tree house in no time. My grandfather had built it for me, many summers ago. One bright spot left behind. It was the perfect distance away from the house. I could escape there. I felt like I was in my own world, but I was close enough to hear them call me to come inside at dinnertime.

I was always losing track of time. Sometimes I fell asleep with a pencil in my hand. My grandmother would make her way all the way out there. She would sound her birdcall straight up the ladder, sending me ten feet into the air. She would laugh every time. I would scowl at her every time.

I loved writing out here. This guy, he knew me better than I knew myself, I feared.

Chace let me climb up first before he made his way half

way up, and then handed me the guitar case so he could travel the rest of the way. I grabbed it and set it on the old wooden floor, then looked around.

The small space looked the same as it had so many years ago, though a bit smaller. My old futon still sat against the wall. Clean blankets covered it. A small end table was next to it. On the other side was an old school house desk. Another spot I loved to write. I walked over to it and sat down.

"I used to come out here all the time," I said. I ran my hand over the surface in front of me. Two windows were on the walls around me, letting the grey rainy light inside. Everything was dusty.

Chace walked over to the futon and sat down. "Your brother and I used to come play out here," he said.

"I miss my grandmother," I said, suddenly. I mourned my lost relationship with her. The closeness we once shared. When I moved away, my relationship with her suffered the most. I didn't call. I didn't want my grandfather to pick up. For a dark while, I blamed her too. I wondered how she could have been so blind to the evil living inside her husband.

"Have you spoken to her recently?" Chace picked up his guitar and started strumming idly, leaning back.

I turned sideways in my seat and faced him. I rested my elbows on my knees and placed my chin in my palms. "I flew down to Florida a couple years ago. The whole family had Christmas."

It was the last time I had seen her. I felt guilty in her presence. My absence at her husband's funeral caused me guilt, no matter the circumstance. I needed to fly down to see her soon, to mend.

Chace stopped playing and looked up at me. "You left something here, you know."

"I did?" I asked.

"I found your notebooks," he answered.

"I know, you told me. My stories." I turned and faced forward in the seat again, stretching my feet out in front of me.

"No, not those." His voice was soft. He looked down at his hand, still strumming.

"What do you mean?" I turned my head back his direction.

"It's like I said with my ex," he stopped playing. "I'm not into games. I always want to be straight with you." He set the guitar on the ground and crossed his arms over his chest. I could tell he was bracing himself for something, then he spoke again.

"I read what you wrote as a teenager. Not just the stories your mom gave us. After your grandparents moved, your mom brought us out here as she packed stuff up and did repairs. She put me in your room, your old room, like I am now. She said to start packing the books, to move to the library. So I did. I was cleaning out stuff from under your bed and I saw a loose floorboard."

He paused so I could process the words. I knew what he found. I didn't think anyone ever would find them. He saw from my face that I knew.

"I think I wanted you before I even knew what it was like to want someone," he began. "I was a kid. I saw your pictures all over your mom's house. I couldn't tell Andrew how beautiful I thought his sister was. I felt ashamed for reading your words when it was obvious they were ones you meant to keep hidden. Ones you hoped no one would ever lay an eye on. I started falling for you through your words. I never expected I'd meet you. You didn't feel real to me. When I found out you were moving back here, to live in this house with me I freaked out a bit. Your mother never knew I found your poetry. I loved reading it. I fell in love. I could escape in them. I wasn't the skinny kid with a broken family missing a leg. I was whoever I wanted to be. I fell in love with your voice, with the brokenness you owned, too. The first time I saw a picture of you on the mantle, I thought I really fell in love. I was, like, 12 I think. Then you hit it big. You made this career out of a dream you had. So, I thought maybe I could have one of my own. That there was more to life than this shitty thing that happened to me. And what happened to you. I was no longer going to let it define me like my father was."

I stared down at my hands. I was in shock. I didn't know what to say. I wasn't angry at him. He was just a kid when he found the truth in my journals, and kids were curious by nature. If it had been me, I would have done the same. I blushed at the thought of him reading my words. My poetry was so raw. Then I felt sick. He knew. He knew the truth. I shoved the thought back down.

His words burned into me. *I think I wanted you before I even knew what it was like to want someone.* He had wanted me for years. He knew what happened to me and he still wanted me. The knowledge that I would be living with him had freaked him out. I remembered his shy smile the day I met him.

This kind of shit didn't happen in real life. It happened in the silly stories I wrote as a child. It happened in Disney movies and romantic comedies. What was my life? Those pages. Fuck...

"Where are they?" My low voice echoed in the small space. I felt a tear trickle down my cheek. I wiped it away before he could see.

Chace motioned to the desk. I slowly reached for the cubbyhole beneath my ass. My fingers found leather and worn pages. I pulled my hand back as if I had been bitten. I wasn't ready. I didn't want to see the words, to imagine him reading them. I bit my lip, still at a loss.

"I'm sorry," he offered. He was genuine. He meant it.

"I'm not mad. Actually, *I'm* sorry." I chuckled running my hands over my face. I didn't know how to feel. I felt anxiety crawling up my throat. I choked it down.

"What for?" he asked.

"That you had to read that. I never showed my poetry to anyone, because it's the writing of mine I am the most unsure of." I felt more exposed on those pages than I ever did, bare, in front of a man.

"Nothing compares to your poetry," he stated. "I'm not saying your other writing is bad. That's not what I mean. You're an amazing writer. But your poetry. It's you. I know that writer's block was killing you, but the words were always there. I changed the day I read those words."

He looked down at his feet and laughed. I had changed into rain boots, but he hadn't. He was wearing a pair of converse. He was always wearing converse. I had a couple pairs, but he had many. I always laughed when I saw a new color. Today he was wearing bright green high tops, untied.

"It's right here," he said.

"What is?" I asked, squinting in the light, narrowing my eyes at his shoes.

He smiled, looking a little embarrassed. "I write dates on them. On my shoes. My old black ones, the ones that are falling apart, I wrote the day my sister died on them. I will never forget the day my world changed. I don't need it there to remember, but I write it back in when it gets rubbed off. Every black pair I get. It was a black day. I have a pair with the date I met your brother on them. A pair with the day I graduated high school. The day I wrote my first song. I carry them over, when it's time to throw one away. This pair has the day I found your poetry on them."

"Why green?" I asked, mesmerized.

"Green, for me, is about becoming new again. I could breathe again when I read your words. I believed I could grow after reading them, despite my past. I felt hope."

We sat silent for a moment. He waited for me to think about his words. Again, I didn't know what to say. Eventually he cut in again. "I'm glad you decided to come back here. I'm glad it has helped." He smiled, and I knew I had to tell him.

"It hasn't," I said, never wavering from his eyes.

His forehand wrinkled. "But you said you're writing? I

know you have been."

"It's not this place though. It's *you*."

I didn't want him to say anything. I wanted him to get off that futon, come over to me and kiss me. To put me out of my misery. These small walls were closing in. The scent of him, his confession, my own, my past, it was choking me. I needed his lips, his hands, I needed him to breathe into me. I needed something to calm me. To make me feel clean.

He stayed still. His light eyes burning into my own. We stayed like that for a while. Finally I broke the current. I looked down at my hands and at my notebook. I heard Chace move around, then the sound of his guitar lightly filled the space again. I looked at him, he was looking down. He spoke low.

"I don't want to play games. So many women just want what they can't have. I'm a simple guy. When I like a girl, I ask her out. When the feeling is gone, we don't go out anymore. I know you're a little caught up in how this looks instead of how it feels, but I know I'm not alone in this."

"No, you're not," I whispered.

"Okay then," he paused. "Come sit over here with me. Let's just write."

April 16th

Over the next week, I had no alone time with Chace. After class and work, he had Aiden over. The boy's mother had taken extra shifts and needed someone to watch him. I got to know the child pretty well. He was loud but polite and funny. The three of us ate and cooked dinner together. A couple nights Kat joined us.

I informed her of everything that had transpired with my roommate. She became a vocal "Team Chace" member. I spent lunches with her dissecting every move he made and what it meant. I felt like we were teenagers again, examining our crush's movements and words, tearing every sentence apart.

Once, while we prepared dinner, Chace walked by me to get milk from the fridge and lightly touched the back of my arm, sending lightning through me. He smiled as he walked back, knowing.

I would explode if I did not get alone time with him to figure everything out. The only thing that eased the tension was our nearly constant texting. We asked each other questions, we offered truths, and it thrilled me.

One thing I had learned about him was that he played hockey but didn't have time to lately with his crazy work schedule.

Now that that was over, he would be playing again in an adult league. He wanted to find time to teach Aiden to skate as well. I was always finding new things to admire about him. He didn't let anything hold him back.

I began hounding my brother about his band's gigs. He informed me they had a gig lined up, one for this weekend. I asked Kat if she wanted to go. And Chace. I planned to stay sober. I didn't want Chace to have any excuse for not kissing me this time. I never wanted anything so bad.

I started riding my new bike up and down the driveway to relieve the tension. I also wrote. I had found a new confidence in my poetry due to Chace and his words. He had read them. He had loved them. I wrote now, for him and for myself. I wanted him to read the new words he had inspired.

When Saturday evening finally rolled around, I was a ball of nerves again. It was worse than the previous week. This time I knew something would happen. Chace and I picked Kat up at her apartment and met Andrew and the band at the bar where they were playing.

Chace couldn't have looked any more desirable. When he came downstairs in a dark grey fitted t-shirt, dark denim, and white converse, my stomach somersaulted.

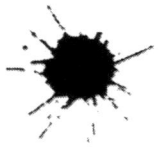

A table close to the stage was reserved for us at the bar. Again, I found Kat on her phone a lot leading up to the show. I wanted to ask her who she is talking to, but couldn't in front of everyone. I wondered if she had a new man in her life, and felt a sting. I wanted there to be one but I would be hurt if she didn't feel like she could share that with me. I had poured out every feeling I had about Chace. Knowing me, I wasn't giving her a moment to even open up about her own romance. I had such a bad habit of not being the kind of person others felt they could confide in. I hoped this wasn't also true with my best friend.

The bar was packed with a lot of women. The band, all very attractive, had a large group of females surrounding them before the show. Chace joined them as soon as we were seated and with drinks. I only planned on having one.

I immediately recognized one female amongst the many. Chace's ex. She was chatting up the drummer while he set up. When she noticed Chace, she cut the conversation short and approached him. I watched them, jealousy swirling, despite my best efforts. I nudged Kat, she leaned towards me.

"That's Chace's ex," I whispered.

"Oh," she mouthed, casually observing them. The conversation seemed to be light. It didn't last long. Chace excused himself and made his way to my brother. A deeper conversation formed between them, their heads were low, excluding those around them.

I wondered if my brother knew anything about us. Not that there was an "us." Chace made his way back to our table, the band headed to the stage, and the lights lowered. My brother reached for the microphone.

"Hey everyone! Thanks for coming out. We're BTPCM. Enjoy!"

A large roar erupted from the crowd. I looked at Chace with a question on my face.

"Band That Plays Country Music!" He yelled over the crowd, smiling widely. "Andrew picked the name."

I laughed loudly and fell back into my seat. It shouldn't have surprised me at all. It was so him. I turned around in my seat, taking in the sea of people. They really knew how to pack them in. I enjoyed live music immensely. I always ended up having a crush on the singer, that would obviously not be the case with this performance, but I expected it would be the case for many in the room.

My brother was easy on the eyes. He stood over six feet tall, was slender yet built, had shaggy light brown hair, and crystal blue eyes. When he began singing, I added "beautiful voice" to his traits.

Kat was enraptured, I could tell. I recalled the fun she had with him last weekend. If she developed a crush on my little brother, I would have mixed emotions. That was a given. Chace, beside me, so close, was tapping his foot. I focused on the lyrics, wondering when he wrote them. Wondering if they were about his ex. I found her in the crowd. Her eyes were focused on me. They quickly flew to the stage when she caught my own.

I focused mine there again as well. My breath caught when I felt Chace's hand reach for mine, where it rested on the edge of my seat, below the table. I turned to him. His gaze flickered to mine briefly, then back to the stage. So, I did the same.

He began slowly running his fingers along my own. Back and forth, lightly. My breath left me. I clenched my legs. He was doing things to me with a barely-there touch that others had been unable to do tangled with me between the sheets.

I focused ahead, trying not to make noise. His hand found my knee, bare. I internally patted myself on the back for wearing a skirt. His fingers traced circles on my skin in time with the music. I tried to listen to the words, but I couldn't hear anything but my own heart.

Andrew's band was amazing, but I wanted this concert to end. Now. I wanted to be alone with this man. My lips parted as his hand went a bit higher, in my peripheral I saw him notice, his hand clenching at the sight. His eyes traveled down, to my chest, to the heavy up and down of my breathing.

Then, he pulled his phone out and began texting. Who could he be texting right now? His left hand never stopped moving on my thigh. My phone lit up on the table. Chace's name appeared. I snatched it up before Kat could see.

Chace: You're killing me...
Me: What the fuck do you think you're doing to me?
Chace: This week has been torture. All I have been able to think about is touching you. Then you wear this skirt. You. Are. Killing. Me.
Me: You're doing the same to me. And death never looked so fucking beautiful.

He laughed at my last text. My foul mouth was coming out and I was being cheesy. I finished my drink, my only drink, and headed for the restroom. I mourned the feeling of his hand falling from my lap. I felt him watch me as I walked away. It burned.

I walked into the restroom, finding the sink immediately. I splashed cold water on neck then headed for an opened stall. I needed a moment. I put the seat down and sat there to catch my breath.

I heard the bathroom door open again, an unknown number of giggling girls entered. The smell of alcohol followed. I tuned them out, staring at my phone and the texts between Chace and me until I heard my name outside the stall. My pen name. My focus went to the girls.

"Yeah. She writes those porn novels. I can't believe he would be interested in her." I had one guess as to who that was. Chace's ex. Another voice chimed in.

"Did he say he is? Isn't she like in her thirties or something? What a cradle robber."

"Yeah. I guess he likes them old now." Charming girl.

"Don't sweat it. Maybe she will head back to New York soon. Good riddance. He doesn't need someone like that. He needs a good Christian girl like you. He'll figure it out."

I was reminded once again I was in the Bible belt where many frowned upon my work. I had received some stares in my time home. I decided to meet the little gossipers head on. I was still giddy from Chace's touch and my drink.

I pushed open the stall door and walked over to the sink next to the ex. Her friend stared over her shoulder. Eyes wide. I washed my hands and turned to her back. Tapping my finger on her shoulder.

"Hi," I beamed as she turned to me. "Just so you know, I don't plan on going back to New York. I like it here. I like the company. I like Chace. Chace likes me. Time to move on."

I walked away, the sound of my boots echoing in the silent bathroom. I waved as I left the restroom.

I headed straight for the bar, and waited for the two girls to emerge. I flagged down the bartender and pointed them out. I handed over a wad of cash, asking that he make sure they did not drive home drunk. I turned to see Chace staring at me. Then glancing at his ex, then back to me, a question was there in his eyes. I turned my head to the side and smiled.

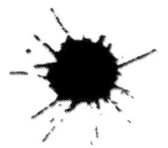

The rest of the concert was amazing. I was so proud of my brother and Chace. I paid more attention to his lyrics for the rest of the night. His hand immediately found mine once I returned to my seat. He had me flustered once more. He would let go for minutes at a time, only to reach for me again. My body, a roller-coaster of emotions, was on the brink.

Kat drank quite a bit. She swayed in her seat with the music, enjoying herself. I noticed Andrew wink at her once during the show, I turned to Kat and questioned her with my eyes. She just rolled them at me, playing off the flirtation. I was beginning to suspect them more and more. After the show, we hung around as the band signed autographs and talked with fans.

After we dropped Kat off, Chace's jeep was silent. His hand reached over to mine and held it firmly. I stared out the window, my hair whipping in the breeze, and smiled. We drove down the driveway slowly.

The April air was warm. Leaves were growing quickly on the trees, flowers were blooming all around the house. My heart beat faster as the house came into view. Chace parked and I quickly jumped out, heading for the porch. He cut me off, grabbing my hand and leading me towards the large pond on the property. A small deck jettisoned out into the water. We walked on the wood to the end and sat. He laid back, so I did too.

The stars were bright, a full moon shone in the sky, illuminating us. Chace turned onto his side, facing me and reached over, running his fingers along the skin exposed between my shirt and skirt. I parted my lips, sighed, and closed my eyes. His hand left me and my eyes flew open, he reached over and brushed the hair from my ear, exposing my neck. I closed my lids again, and turned my head to the side. Once again inviting his lips to my neck. Knowing this time he would accept the offer.

He spoke then, his soft voice, hushed, I turned, to hear him better. He was staring at the hand lightly tracing my skin.

"I saw you on T.V. last year. I remember. That day I went to drop some music off with your brother. He was so excited. His sister was going to be at the Oscars. So I watched that night. I wanted to see more than just the pictures from the house and the ones in magazines. You were wearing that white dress. Your hair was pulled up. I had never seen anyone more beautiful."

He stopped, pointing down to his shoes. I looked.

White converse, with the date I walked down the red carpet with Tristan, written in black ink. I closed my eyes, and he continued.

"I wrote so many songs about you. That dress. Your hair. Your skin. But here, the way you look to me right now...that doesn't compare to this. To the way you feel. I know it sounds silly. I never thought I could be the kind of guy to have a woman like you turn his way. I broke up with my ex when I found out you were coming here. Not that I thought I had a chance, but being with someone when you have these, these thoughts, it's not fair. I just wanted to be free. I want to know everything about you. Not just the pretty things, the dark, the dirt. And I want you to see mine."

I couldn't speak. I couldn't move. I opened my eyes and stared at his own, they were trained on his hands. I willed him to look at me. He finally did, and he held my gaze.

"What are you thinking?"

I could barely think with his words and his hands on me.

"I'm just trying to figure out if you're real," I managed. "Or if I just wrote you in my head, then placed you in my life to deal."

His lips found mine, and I died. It started light, then quickened. His body pressed against mine, his hand found the apex of my leg, pulling it around him; I pressed my heel into him, as I pushed myself into him. He groaned into my mouth. I pulled my mouth from his, and he quickly moved to my neck.

I started repeating four words repeatedly, *'tell me you're real'* in between inaudible sounds and curse words. His answer came once, *'I am'*.

He trailed his lips and tongue down my neck, to the neckline of my shirt; I laid my head back gasping, as his hand traveled from the hold on my knee, up my thigh, beneath my billowy skirt. He rolled onto me, settling between my thighs, my skirt fell down around me, the slight chill of the air left goosebumps everywhere.

When his hands found the lace underneath I grabbed his neck, pulling his mouth to mine once again, begging him to continue.

I was filled with conflicting forces. Arousal and anxiety. I was often a fan of the big three. First kiss, foreplay, fucking. Intimacy was not in the cards with me. Best to get it all over with, then on to the writing. It was my M.O. I was dangerously close to repeating it. I didn't want to move too fast with Chace. My body needed to quit being so bossy.

I gasped as his fingers suddenly entered me. I gripped his shirt, my nails digging into his back. They quickly left me, as his mouth did as well. He pressed his forehead to mine and whispered, "I'm sorry. Too much. Too much."

I shook my head to agree against him. "Don't stop touching me," I begged. I reached his mouth again. Needing him. I stuck my hand under the back of his shirt, tugging upwards, he pulled away from me long enough to reach behind him, yanking it over his shoulders.

He took my hands from his body, raised them over my head, and secured them with one hand. His lips found the tattoo starting at my wrist; he traced his tongue along the script. He found each visible bit of poetry, and claimed them with his warm lips.

I chanted each poem that was forever on my flesh, in my mind, as he branded them. He lifted my shirt, finding the script upon my ribcage, below my bra, and I became dizzy. I focused on the stars above, poetry screaming inside. His hand still secured my wrists, I was helpless, and I arched my back off the deck. He traveled lower, to the prose on my thigh, tracing each word. I clenched at the nearness of his mouth, the desperate need for him to taste me.

Why was I fighting sex? Couldn't we just give in? My mind and body went round and round, they were both beat up, and which would win would surely be determined by the beautiful man kissing every word on my body, swirling new ones inside.

I pushed him back, confusion threaded his face as I found my way to my knees, I pressed against his bare chest. He was all hard lines and soft voice. I was undone. I pushed him onto his back and took him in. The beauty of him. It was a full moon, and his ivory skin burned into me. He had no words to read, no verse to place my lips on, but I didn't need it.

I pressed my lips to his neck, and relished the sigh it brought forth. I took my time, tasting him, touching him, coaxing music from his mouth.

April 17th

I woke in a tangle of limbs as the sun rose. It had been so long since someone had shared my own bed and not a hotel room or their bed. I always hated having someone invade my own space, it always gave me anxiety. I pulled my right hand up to my chest and pressed. My heart beat low and slow, no panic lived there.

We had come so close to going all the way the night before. We were rushed breath, sweat, and raw desire. We both somehow managed to stop ourselves. I was glad we had. I wasn't ready.

I couldn't believe the thoughts swimming in my head. I wanted something of substance with this young man. Something real. Something new. Using him was not in the cards. I didn't know where to go from here. It was foreign to me.

One-night stands littered my past. With Tristan, it was easy. We never had to deal with the day-to-day mess that came with a commitment. There was no fear of our romance becoming monotonous. We never saw each other enough for it to get to that point.

I knew why I was able to commit to Tristan. It wasn't because of the way the world saw him. It wasn't his beauty, his talent, or his spark. It was the knowledge that a commitment to him still held the promise of my freedom. It was easy.

Would I be able to really commit to Chace? I wanted it. I wanted to grow up. I wanted a true adult relationship. I looked over at him, still sleeping. He took my breath away.

He was on his stomach, the sheet down around his waist. His broad shoulders were silk under my fingers. His artificial leg peaked from the comforter.

He hesitated when we undressed to sleep next to each other. I saw it in his eyes and felt it in his hands. There was not an inch of him I didn't wish to touch, even those places he feared would diminish my desire. I kissed him, hard, easing his jeans down, reassuring him. We explored each other again in the warmth of my bed. I stripped down to my undergarments, as did he. His mouth found every bit of my skin that was exposed, not just the words, and I returned in kind. We continued until our hands and limbs slowed, sleep claiming us. He succumbed first. I watched him sleep; the gentle movement of his chest hypnotized me.

I eventually fell too, tucked into his side. I recalled his words, his words before the kiss. I didn't think he loved me. But I knew he could. I didn't deserve it, but I was going to fucking take it.

I slipped from the sheets and padded over to my vanity, grabbing my notebook and pen. The art of him in my bed at sunrise…it needed to be put on paper.

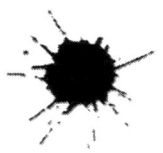

There was to be another get together at the house that day. My mother wanted to barbecue. Hamburgers, hotdogs, potato salad, the works.

After writing a bit, I slipped into the shower. Leaving the poetry on the bed next to Chace. When I entered the room again, he was gone, as was the paper. I saw a text from him on my phone.

Chace: Last night. Yes. It was all of that. I don't know how to act normal today when your family comes over. But I'll try.

I smiled at the screen and bit my lip. I was probably blushing too. I had turned into a 16-year-old girl again. I tossed my phone on the bed, grabbed my iPad and began attending to my social media and emails.

I found one from my assistant titled 'Tristan', and my stomach flipped. It was not the name I wanted to see now. I opened it, and found a link to an article on People Magazine's website. I didn't want to click. Why was she sending me this? Could she sense I was finding something, with someone new? I am such a fucking masochist. I clicked.

The article stated that Tristan's romance with his costar had fizzled, and sources close to him speculated that he wanted *me* back. My whereabouts were unknown. Surprising. I may be in the Ozarks but those leeches could find blood anywhere.

My next email was from Gemma. A link to the same article. I fell onto my bed, snatched my phone and checked my texts again. I had one from her.

Gemma: Did you read the article? Tristan called me wanting your new number. I didn't give it to him. Call me ASAP.

Why, why was this happening? I must be at the part of the book where conflict emerged. I guess the honeymoon was over.

I texted Kat and begged her to join in on the barbecue fun. She declined. She was insanely hungover. Damn. We went through a brief play by play of the night. She cheered for me in emoticons. I eye-rolled back.

I made my way downstairs, about an hour before anyone would be showing up. I found Chace in the kitchen. He was preparing hamburger patties. He smiled at my entrance. I bit my lip again.

"You look nice," he breathed.

I was wearing an oversized long sleeve t-shirt, skinny jeans, and ballet flats. My tangle of hair was in a messy knot on the top of my head, and I had opted out of wearing my contacts, choosing my wire frames instead.

He was looking at me as if he saw only the girl in the white dress. He went to the sink, washed his hands, dried them on the towel hanging from the stove and made his way to me.

He placed a finger under my chin and raised my mouth to his. The taste of mint met my tongue. I wrapped my arms around his neck, running my hands through his short brown hair. He splayed his hands upon my back, pressing into me. I raised up on my toes, he was so far away. In my flats, he towered over me by over a foot. He reached down, lifting me onto the counter.

Once again, I used my heel to bring him as close to me as possible as his mouth claimed me. His kiss, it was more than any other man's was. I felt more exposed than I had ever been. His hand found the elastic of my hair band and untangled it, letting the waves fall. He cradled my head, leaning me back, working his way over my neck. This was the best fucking breakfast I had ever had.

The clearing of a foreign but familiar throat stilled our busy hands. I pulled away and looked into Chace's eyes, trained over my shoulder. My brother's voice cut through the kitchen.

"Really guys. It's 10 in the morning. Get a room. You both have one." I rested my forehead on Chace's shoulder. It bounced with his laughter. "I can't believe you're mauling my sister on a Sunday. You knew I was coming over. I think I lost my appetite." He pretended to gag.

I jumped off the counter, punching my brother in the arm. I couldn't believe he was so casual about this. But fuck, I was relieved. I didn't want, whatever this was, to cause turmoil for Chace and my family. They had a great thing going here. I didn't want to be the one to wreck it all. I thought of my mother. I worried she would be a different story. I feared that she would disapprove. I couldn't handle it. I needed him.

Soon, the house filled with voices, food, and laughter. I found myself walking on eggshells. My mind was everywhere. I was fucking manic. Gemma was texting me, wanting to talk about Tristan. I ignored her. I didn't care. I was over getting alerts about him. He could do whatever he wanted. I was over it. Over him.

I wanted to reach out and touch Chace every time he came near me, but didn't. We shared glances though. I caught Andrew rolling his eyes at us more than once. We hadn't talked about what he had interrupted. I wondered if Chace would talk to him more about it. I wondered *what* he would tell him this was.

I finally met Aiden's mother when she stopped to bring her son by for a bit. She was very friendly but seemed exhausted. She had to appreciate Chace so much for all he did to help her.

We didn't play games this Sunday. We simply sat on the back lawn, around the large pond and talked. Chace stood on the deck and threw a large branch into the water over and over again as Artax retrieved it. I tried to keep my eyes away from him. It was difficult.

I could feel summer around the corner, in both my happiness and in the sunshine. I wondered how much I would see here, of this year. I pondered how much longer I would stay in Missouri.

My mother, always one to sense my thoughts, sat next to me and asked, "So, how long do we have left with you, Dear?" She reached for my hand and gently squeezed it.

"I don't know," I answered. "I didn't think long, but, I'm writing again. And I don't want to ruin that. I don't want to change a thing. I don't want to scare it away."

"I like to hear that. It's so nice having you here. Just a short drive away. I miss the Sundays at this house. Remember them?"

"Yes," I smiled. I was fine in the daylight hours. My mother had the warmest smile. I never wanted to be the one to diminish it. "Board games. Reading. Late breakfast and early dinner. I loved it." I was always telling her half-truths.

"Me too. How are things with you and Chace?"

"What do you mean?" I asked, too sharply.

"Are you getting along? I'm sure you see him more. I'm so glad he quit that second job of his. School is the most important thing and lord knows he would have us to help him with anything he needed."

"Yeah. He did work a lot," I replied, relieved. I looked at Chace in the distance. He was sitting on the edge of the dock, his arm around Artax, who was perched next to him.

"I just wish he had more family. Family he could be close with."

"He has us," I said and looked around at everyone. Smiles were surrounding me. "You know he considers you guys as family."

"And you now, too," she added.

"Yeah. I guess. Let's just call me his roommate." Dear God, don't say I'm his family.

My mother stood. "Help me bring the dishes inside."

I rose with her, gathering plates and other items, and retreated into the house. She ran water and began washing. I took my place on the other side to dry. Just like when I was a child.

She handed me a plate and cleared her throat. I looked at her profile. She was gazing out the kitchen window.

"I saw the way you two were looking at each other," she said, evenly.

"What do you mean?" I dried the plate, keeping my voice as even as hers, studying her features.

"It was both of you. You were both glancing at each other and had that look on your faces. Like you think the other hung the moon."

I couldn't tell how she was feeling about this. She was always so good at talking about any situation without letting her emotions enter. It was one reason I was able to go to her for advice so often when I was younger. I couldn't help my denial.

"You're getting delusional in your old age," I joked, nudging her. I turned my eyes back to my task.

"Deny it if you want. I know what I saw. Just be careful."

"With what?" I turned back quickly. I was sure my face gave me away. She was onto us.

"With him," she replied.

"What do you mean? You think the world of him."

"I do. But he doesn't need anyone leaving him heartbroken." Ouch. My own mother. I set down the cup I had been toweling off.

"Mom," I began, carefully. "Are you implying that I'm like, a 'bad girl' or something?"

She wasn't wrong, but how did she know? Phone calls home were always light, about work and travel. Never about men in my life.

"No, Hun. I just know, you've never given any indication that you want to settle down any time soon. I'm okay with that. You take care of yourself and you have this life you have created for yourself that I couldn't be more proud of. But Chace is different."

I began drying the cup again, furiously. "Well none of this conversation is necessary, because he is young and I'm not interested."

The lie stung on my lips. Why the hell had I said that? I was too used to keeping my love life from her.

My mother sighed. "He's young, but not in his soul. Not in his heart. Not like Andrew. He'd match you. He'd challenge you. Honestly, he is the kind of man I would hope you would find one day."

"You're running in circles. Let's just call it. I feel like you're encouraging me to marry the guy and also scaring me away."

"Okay, okay, I'm done," she paused. "He has just had a hard life, Sera. And he is doing so well. Others, they would have let it destroy them. I see it so often. You know how it kills me. Children from harsh backgrounds, letting circumstance and everything turn them down the wrong path. Drugs, stealing, and so many other horrible things. But Chace. He has made a strong life for himself."

"I agree. He really has it together." My stomach was home to an anvil. I had a hard life, but I had kept it from her.

"We all carry scars. He is just really good at hiding his," she said, unknowingly wounding me.

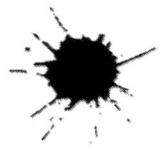

Before long, the house was empty again. Save for two. Before she left, my mother convinced me to do a small book signing at the local library. The town had been abuzz about my arrival since before I landed.

I had managed so far to stay out of the public eye. It was

easy to do in the country. She felt it would be a nice thing to do for the fans I had here. I worried a little that those who felt my work was not acceptable would show up just to stare me down. I ordered a couple hundred books from my publishing house to be sent to my mother's house, where I would sign them for the event.

I retreated to my bathroom as soon as everyone pulled away to take a shower. I let the warm water flow over me and thought of Chace. He was downstairs waiting for me. What would this night bring? My hearth fluttered at the thought.

Once I was clean, I checked my social media once again, anxious, after the mornings findings. I had a new email from my assistant. Another link. I regretfully clicked. It was an Entertainment Weekly article about Tristan, once again discussing his breakup and his apparent pining for me.

A source close to him stated things did not pan out because he was not over me. The source claimed he had simply used the actress to make me jealous and push me into commitment. I wondered who the laughable source was. It was a complete crock of shit. I knew better than to read much into the words. The end of the article claimed I had left New York. Well they go that right. And that Tristan was determined to find me. I didn't believe it. I doubted he gave much thought to my changed number and sudden move.

I slammed my laptop, jumped off the bed and got dressed. I stomped down the stairs and headed into the kitchen, finding Chace cutting some sort of cake.

He smiled. "Where are you going?"

I returned his smile. "Nowhere. Came down to find you." I sat at the bar.

"Would you like a piece?" The treat appeared to be cheesecake.

"Where did that come from?" My eyes widened. "Oh, is that my mother's?" My mother made the most divine New York style cheesecake. Ironically, I never found anything in New York that compared.

"Yes," he smiled, putting a piece on another plate. "She forgot to mention she brought it."

I snatched my plate and dove in. I moaned as soon as the piece hit my mouth. It was like my birthday, and fresh snow on my tongue, and fuzzy slippers. I missed that damn sweet goodness. I found Chace watching me.

"My mother suspects there is something going on between us," I said, around my mouthful of food.

"Really? What did she say?"

"She seemed to be warning me away from you," I said, stabbing my fork into the remainder of my slice. I twisted the fork, and looked up at him. Confusion covered his face.

"Oh."

"Not because of you. Because of me, I think. Because of my past. Since I haven't had many," I hesitated, "relationships."

"I see," he said simply.

"Does that bother you? Maybe it doesn't matter." He made his way around the kitchen island. He grabbed my knee and spun me on my stool. I reached my arm back, set down my fork, and looked up at him and into his honest eyes. He placed his hand on my neck, his thumb tracing my jaw.

"You know, for me, this isn't casual. This isn't just some fling. Messing around." His voice was low, my insides burned.

"I know." He was not a man whose intentions would be doubted. I didn't want another silly fling with him. I wanted more.

"Good," he smiled. I felt relief coming off in waves.

"The same for me. Casual is my specialty." My life. My past. My dirty secret. "But that's not what you are."

He let out a breath. "How did this happen? I can't believe I'm touching you. I feel that way every time I put my hands on you."

He ran his thumb along my jaw, tilting my mouth towards him. I kept my eyes on his. The crystal color of them. Taking it in. Taking everything in that was being said.

"I'm as real as I've ever been, when you do," I breathed.

Then his mouth was on mine. I pushed off the stool, nearly falling off. My hand gripped his neck as he wrapped one arm around me, lifting me to the counter. He fit himself between my thighs, and I pressed him closer within. Everything went crimson.

April 18th

A new week rolled around, with one distinct change: I was deliriously happy. Chace left my bed early for class, kissing my forehead as he left my room. I wanted him in my bed each morning. I wanted him to be the one who erased the memory of me sneaking out of foreign bedrooms at dusk.

I decided to avoid all social media that day. I wanted to remain in my happy bubble, without my ex's shadow blocking my sunlight. I texted Kat to confirm our lunch. I was determined to get to the bottom of things with her.

She was having a busy beginning to her week. New shipments of purses and blouses were due so I promised to pick something up for us so we could sneak a meal in her stock room. I placed her favorite salad on the table surrounded by boxes and sat down with her.

She had a mouth full of greens when I attacked. "So what's going on with you lately?"

"What do you mean?" She cocked an eyebrow at me.

"You just seem distracted. And on your phone..." I pointed to the device. Face down. An inch from her left hand. "A lot."

She blushed at my question. I was on to something.

"Ah. I don't know." She grabbed her phone and slipped it into the outer pocket of her purse.

"Spill it," I demanded and pointed my fork at her.

"There's nothing to spill." She shrugged.

"Yes there is. Come on. Are you seeing someone?"

"No."

"Then what is it? Your ex?"

"No!" She exclaimed. The disgust covering her face made me believe she was serious. "Never, that's done. I can't wait for the divorce to be final."

"See, you seem different about that. You were desolate before. And damn, don't get me wrong, I'm happy you're not. But what changed?"

"Okay," she said, sitting back and staring at the ceiling. "Just don't get all weird about this." She leaned forward again, put her fork down, and reached for a napkin.

"Kat. I'm currently kind of seeing the dude I live with who is like family to my family and seven years younger than me. Spill it."

She took a breath. "Well. I have been talking to this guy. Texting. That's it." She blushed and stared at her food.

"Who is it?" Did she meet him on social media? Surely people didn't use Tinder around here. All you would find were people you had known since preschool.

"I don't know," she edged.

"What do you mean? Like is he from a dating website or something?" She wasn't giving me much to work with here.

"No. Ugh." She leaned back in her chair again and crossed her arms. "This is going to sound too weird when I say it. Okay. I got a text from a wrong number a while back. I said they had the wrong person. No big deal. Then they texted me again. And we, we started talking."

"What? How does that even happen?" This was how you ended up on Dateline. This was how you ended up stuffed into a freezer. This was how you ended up a skin suit!

"I don't even know. He wanted to talk to someone and he said he thought it would be easy to talk to me, since we didn't know each other. Since we were strangers. We have been sharing everything. I told him all about my divorce. He has told me about his problems. He called me a week ago. We don't even know each other's names. Who knows if we will ever meet. And we may, and have absolutely no attraction to each other. But, regardless, he has helped me."

She seemed relieved to have it out there. The way I did when I showed her my poetry.

"Oh wow," I said, still processing. "I don't even know what to say. I've never heard of anything like that." I kind of wish I had thought of it. It would make for a good story.

"I know." She sat back up and reached for her phone. "Weird, huh? And I'm sorry I didn't tell you. I just didn't want to share it yet. I'm sorry." He face was still a bit pink, and it was adorable.

"Stop apologizing. You're my best friend, but, I know I've been gone. I know it isn't like when we were kids. I do, I do want us to be that close again."

"But you're going to leave here one day again, right?"

"I don't know."

I didn't want to think about the future. A future with leaving, anyway. Initially, I had no desire to stay, and now, staying seemed right. I didn't know what was going on with my love life. It was too new. But I didn't want to put an expiration date on it before it had even begun.

"Because of Chace?" My friend was smiling at me.

"Yeah," I smiled back. "I think. I don't know. Who knows what is even happening? But, I feel like I can be me with him. Or no, not me, a *better* version of myself. Someone worthy of him. Because who I was, she couldn't keep a man like that."

"You're too hard on yourself. Stop that." She threw a carrot at me, and I ducked.

"No, I was shitty. I don't want to be that person anymore." I wanted to crawl out of this skin, shed it, and begin again. It was never too late to begin again, right? I had to believe that.

"Well I don't want to be who I was before, either." She finished her salad and threw it into the trash across the room. Then came back and sat down.

"What the hell are you talking about? You are perfect," I said, still working on my lunch.

"Well, maybe, I want to be a bit like you now."

"Why would you want that?" I choked on the bite in my mouth.

"I want to be a little more selfish. I want to do the things *I* want. I don't want to take care of someone. I want to be a little reckless. I never was. It's my turn."

"Proceed with caution," I laughed. "My mother suspects something is going on. And I didn't exactly get the impression she was thrilled."

"You're mom supports whatever you do." My friend's motherly, advice-giving voice had emerged. "You know that. But, like you said, he is like family to them. So it may take some adjusting."

"I know." I hoped the adjusting would be easy, painless.

"Is it worth it? You and Chace?"

I did not hesitate. "Yes."

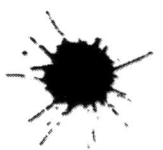

The very next day, Chace and I had a cycling date. An early morning cycling date. I groaned into my pillow, regretting my agreement. I had been meeting him in town when he had breaks between classes to ride. Today he would not have much time so we decided to ride just after six in the morning. He knew I was not a morning person, and that I was agreeing just to appease him. His smile declared his appreciation.

I hoped that Chace wasn't one of those people who cycled regardless of the elements. Rain, shine, snow, hail, nothing could stop him. He didn't seem like the type of guy to let it stop him. I hoped he was aware his cycling partner would let that stuff stop her, gladly. I fumbled in the early morning light for my phone and tapped out a text to him, inquiring if our trip was still on. If he said no then I would gladly head back off to dream land. My phone dinged quickly, alerting me to his response. We were still on. Wishful thinking always bit me in the ass.

I stumbled out of bed, showered, and made my way downstairs in proper attire. Chace was loading our bikes onto the rack on the back of his jeep. He had a thermos in his hand when he reached me. He knew I needed it.

We rode silently into town, comfortable in each other's presence. I needed to talk to my mother. This was feeling familiar and I was happy. Strangely, the fact that we still had not slept together had me feeling something close to falling. *It's all in the fall.*

After a quick ten-mile ride, we headed home so that he could get ready for class. I wouldn't see him until he got home that night. He had a shift at the local bakery and coffee shop after class. I took a quick morning nap when we returned, texting my mother before I hit the sheets asking if I could meet her for lunch that day. I texted Kat as well telling her today was the day. She wished me luck.

I met my mother at the only sushi joint nearby. Their rolls were surprisingly good. Nothing compared to New York, but I enjoyed them. My mother had become a fan of sushi when she came to visit me one fall.

My mother was on me as soon as the waitress was gone

with our drink order. "So, what's up?" She knew. She always knew. I tried to keep my face blank, to hide the freight train of fear inside.

"Well," I began, slowly. "I wanted to talk to you about something. I'm scared. I'm not going to lie mom. I'm scared of how you will react."

"You know that you can tell me anything," she assured. "You always can." She reached across the table and patted my hand.

"I know that. I just, don't like letting you down..." She surely wouldn't be too surprised. She had already suspected.

"What is it?" She asked.

"There's something going on with Chace and I." Bandage off.

"I see," she said, focused on the menu. She knew what she was going to order but still, her eyes were trained on it. I wanted to crawl into a hole.

"So, what do you think?" I said after a minute, an hour, a day of silence.

"I'm not surprised." She set her menu down. "I told you I noticed something on Sunday. I knew you were brushing off the truth. You're both adults. Whether this pans out or not I will love you both. You know, there is the age difference. I know you are a smart girl. I know you are not blind to that. Just remember it. Don't get too caught up in looks or lust or whatever."

"Mom, don't say lust." I groaned.

"You've said far worse in your books."

"True." She got me there. But she was my mom. My teacher-mom. I didn't want her saying lust.

"Just. Be careful." She smiled lightly at my confused face. "Be careful with him."

"I don't intend to hurt him."

"How many people do? Doesn't stop people from being hurt."

I wondered if she was thinking about my dad. He didn't give two shits about hurting us, so many years ago. Her father didn't give two shits about hurting me, but she still loved him. Because I couldn't break her heart with the ugly truth.

"I'm not going to," I said, my voice was firm.

"Does this mean you're staying around?"

"Yes. As long as there is something here, between him and me, I don't see me leaving. I know that sounds crazy. I don't even know what this is. But I don't want to leave."

With those words, I had made a decision. I couldn't decide if it was me still being reckless or if it was me finally growing up.

"So you do care about him, then?" She smiled and my shoulders relaxed. I had been tense since the moment we sat down.

"I do. He's not what I deserve. I want him though."

"You deserve the best. Don't let yourself think otherwise." She reached across the table and took my hand again.

"I love you."

"And I, you."

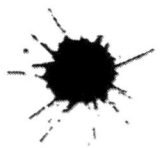

I waited on the porch for Chace to make it home that night. I lit some candles, poured a glass of wine, and pulled out my type-writer. I wrote for two hours before I saw his headlights shining down the long driveway. Artax barked until he parked, as usual. He knew who it was. But he barked all the same.

I gulped down the last of my drink, and set my typer to the side. I propped my bare legs onto the wicker table in front of me. I studied the ink there, as I waited. Chace smiled at me as he came up the front steps, and then pointed inside. He needed a minute. My phone dinged next to me. I pulled up a text from my New York pal.

Gemma: you need to call me! Tristan came looking for me. He begged for your number. I wouldn't give it to him but I let it slip you went home. CALL ME!

Great. I would call her in the morning. I didn't believe he would track me down here. It was ridiculous. Gemma was very dramatic. Truly she just wanted to gossip about the situation. I turned my phone to silent and set it aside as Chace returned.

"I talked to my mom about us today," I blurted. The wine making me brave.

"How'd that go?" He sipped his beer and stared into the yard.

"Weird at first," I admitted. "Then, good. She's still worried I am going to break your heart."

He turned back to me and looked me in the eye. "I'll take my chances."

I blushed. "I guess I can't be upset that people worry about my commitment issues."

"She's probably just thinking of my mother when she says that."

"Your mother?" I didn't know much about her, besides the fact that she had torn his family apart. I didn't know anything about who she was before that night.

"Yeah," he said, evenly. He took a seat on the chair next to me, and stared into the distance again. "I hated my mom, for so many years. I hated what she did to us. I hated that she took my sister from us, and nearly took me out as well. But, she was my mother. I still have memories of her. Good memories. I remember her taking my sister and me for gelato. I remember her sitting in a chair on the porch watching us ride bikes back and forth, never losing site of us. I remember her reading to me at night, and kissing me on the forehead before she pulled the covers tight. She would whisper 'night tiger' and I loved that. I loved her. It's hard for me to reconcile that with what she did. Even after all of these years. I could have died too. There were times I wish I had, so I could have just gone wherever my sister went. I hated what she did to my father, hated what he turned into. He was never the same. The sight of me reminded him of everything he lost. The sight of where my leg had been. He shut me out. He shut down, when I needed him the most." His voice was so low; I could barely make out the last part.

"I'm so sorry." I reached for his hand, dangling over the armrest. I gently touched my fingertips to his.

I knew how he felt. Some small part of me had loved my grandfather for years, and I hated myself for it. The guilt ripped at me. He had destroyed the innocent girl I was, but I remembered little things he did to make me happy. I would smile at those thoughts, and then spend days punishing myself for letting any love inside that remained, free. I clenched my eyes at the memory of it all and shook my head. I focused on Chace again.

"One day I went to my dad's study to let him know I wanted to go ride my bike," he started. "I didn't enter right away because I heard him talking. He was on the phone and the door was cracked. I didn't listen in on my dad's conversations, but I couldn't stop myself. The first thing I heard him say was 'Jesus, Sheila. She was having an affair. With a man who didn't want kids.' I stopped. He was talking to his sister about my mother. He had found emails of hers. She hated her life with my father. She didn't love him. She was planning to leave him and us when we got back from our vacation. She didn't want to commit. She never wanted a family or kids."

Fuck. His mother and my father would have made a perfect pair. I gripped his hand harder. No words came to me. He turned to me.

"I'm not saying you're like that," he insisted. "I'm not saying your mom thinks you are. But, maybe, she stills sees that little boy she helped. And damn, she did help me. She was the mother I wished I could have been born with. But I'm an adult now. I can make my own choices. If I get my heart broken, it's okay. That's life. It's ugly and petty and harsh. But I've survived the worst. So have you."

"You're so…" I stopped. I hoped he saw himself the way I did. The way everyone did. "I don't know. You are ridiculous. You're wonderful. You're fucking perfect."

"I think that about you. Especially when you cuss like a sailor." He gripped my hand back.

"I'm a classy lady." We both laughed.

Nineteen

April 20th

So, this was it. This is what I wrote about from time to time. This is what I loved reading about: sharing the sunrise with a man you didn't want to leave. The art of him, in my bed, at sunrise. Fuck. He was lying there, dead to the world. His lips lightly parted, as he breathed. *It's all in the fall.* I was falling. Too fast, but it didn't make it any less true. And strangely, in that moment, I felt no fear.

I left him sleeping. I wrote a note and slipped out, again. I was meeting my mother early at her house before the book signing she had organized that day. My novellas had arrived at her house; I still needed to sign them. I couldn't stop smiling. I was an idiot.

The library was a complete mad house. I was not expecting it in my small hometown. They must have come from every county in the area. I didn't know my mother had put much of a word out. I had been worried about the turnout and the attitude, but everyone was wonderful. Everything was falling together.

To my surprise, when I addressed everyone beforehand, I announced that I would be publishing a collection of poems later that year. I hadn't discussed it with my agent or publishing company. They would be less than thrilled with my rogue approach.

Nevertheless, Chace made me crazy. Crazy in my belief that people would embrace it and follow me in my new endeavors.

The only bad seed of the day was Chace's ex. She showed up at the signing, to my surprise. She was with a friend who clutched one of my books. She never came to my table, but rather, gave me the stink eye the entire time. I couldn't help but laugh inside. I felt for her, I did. Losing a guy like that had to sting.

After nearly five hours of signing, well past the allotted time, things began to wrap up. I ran to the bathroom while the library staff and my mother began to tidy up. I had been holding it for nearly an hour.

When I returned, I found a small crowd around my table again. Possible latecomers. They were whispering and excited. I smiled and approached, then stilled at the sight of my mother talking to a man facing away from me.

Her face was white as she glanced around his 6'3" frame in my direction. He turned when he saw her notice my approach. It. Was. Tristan. Fucking fuckedy fuck FUCK.

My stomach lurched. He turned back, said something to my mother, and then walked to me. He smiled.

"How did you find me?" I didn't want him smiling at me. I didn't want to smile at him. I didn't want to have small talk. The crowd had turned their attention to us.

"Wait. Save it. Come with me." I grabbed his arm and pulled him into the women's restroom. Locking the door behind us. "Okay. Spill it."

"Your assistant is dating my publicist now," he said. His green eyes made me angry. He had a strange look in them. Affection.

"Wow, she didn't tell me that. And I can assure you it is an ex-assistant now." I made a mental note to fire her once this conversation was over.

"Come on, Ser. Don't take it out on her," he said, walking

towards me. I backed up, hitting the door behind me. I pointed my finger at him, causing him to stop.

"Okay, I'll take it out on you. First, don't call me that. Second, what the hell are you doing here?" I screeched. I hated that he had me all worked up.

"I miss you," he said. He had the gall to sound sincere. He had won an Oscar a few years ago though.

I pulled a deep breath through my nose. "No, no you don't."

"I fucked up," he apologized. "I wasn't thinking. I never should have let you go, and I never should have ended it the way that I did." He stared at me full on with his deep forest eyes. Women got lost in them. I just wanted to tear them out of his big dumb attractive head. Green eyes were lying eyes.

I aimed a glare at him. "No shit. A text? Mature."

"I'm sorry." Once again with the sincere voice.

"For the shitty way you did it? For moving on so fast? It doesn't matter." I waved my hand in the air, dismissively. "I'm over it." I turned around and reached for the lock. He closed his hand over mine. I pulled away as if I had been burned by him.

"Please, just talk to me." He pulled my hand into his. "I flew all this way."

I ripped it away once more. "Not my fault you're an idiot. And there's nothing to talk about. You live in a world where rumors and speculation are always there. You knew how the tabloids were. And you used them to end it. You couldn't even do it yourself. A relationship without trust is nothing."

My voice was getting steadily louder. "Not just in your world. In the real world. Don't you know what people think of me now? A lot of them hate me. Or feel sorry for me. At least that's how I felt when my Twitter, Facebook, and Instagram feeds were jammed with pissed off fans calling me every name in the book when you were the one who cheated! But just because you're the biggest movie star in the world, they somehow made it out that I wasn't 'woman enough' to keep you. Maybe I wasn't. In your eyes."

"Who cares what they think?" The gentleness in his eyes was sickening. He actually believed the shit coming out of his mouth.

"I did! They think I ran away heartbroken from you and pathetic. That I couldn't stay in New York. Maybe it was true. But the world didn't need to know."

"Is that why you came back here?" He stepped towards me, I stepped back.

"Don't flatter yourself," I tossed the words at him. "I came back here to write. That's what I am: a writer. I want people to remember that. I'm not just the ex-girlfriend of that movie star."

He stared down at his feet and clenched his fists. "You have no idea how much I regret what happened. How much I miss you." His deep voice, even at a whisper, echoed across the small bathroom.

I lowered my voice a little. I had been yelling too much. "Yet, you waited months to come find me."

At the softening of my voice, he looked up. "I had to find you first. I wanted to come to you. I didn't just want to call."

"But a text was suitable to end a year long relationship? The only one I have ever been in." I sighed. "Are you done with filming?"

"Yes," he replied.

I chuckled to myself. "Oh, okay. So, now that you're done with your little fling you want to come back to me. Now that it is getting close to when we begin promoting the last film, you want to patch things up. Well I may not be an actress, but I can pretend to like you just fine for the cameras. We are done here." I huffed.

I made my way around him, widely, and set my sights on the door again. Tristan reached for me. I backed up again, avoiding his touch.

"There's someone else!" I blurted.

"What?" His tone deflated.

"I've met someone else."

"Who?" His voice was loud again.

"It doesn't matter. But you need to go." I pointed to the door he was blocking.

"Who is he?"

"He isn't anyone you know. Just let me out! Please." I felt hysterical. I was in this drama again. I wanted out.

"Who is he?"

"He's just some kid. Now get out of the way." I waved wildly with my hands. I could feel my anxiety kicking up a notch with every word, every breath. I was trapped in a bathroom by a man. A man I didn't want to touch me. If he kept me in here much longer, I was going to throw up on his expensive shoes. My skin itched and my eyes watered.

"Is it serious? I can't leave if it's serious. I won't leave." His voice was determined. I knew how Tristan was when he was determined. There was no stopping him. I had once admired it. Now I hated that trait.

"It isn't serious. It's just a fling. It doesn't mean anything." I was okay with lying to my ex. I didn't owe him the truth. I didn't owe him my heart. I just needed to be out of this situation as quickly as possible before I broke down.

"You're just using him for a story right? Just like the ones before me. I know it was real with us because you didn't write about us." The pleading tone had returned.

"Who told you about that? Wait, my assistant right? Yes. I am writing again because of him. I am writing about him."

"Can we talk when you come back to New York?"

"Yes, fine," I groaned.

I didn't intend to go back, but if that's what he needed to hear to get out of my damn way then fine. Lying to him was of no consequence.

I was more than rattled when I finally made it home that evening. I stopped by Kat's to fill her in. Twitter began to blow up. Someone at the library took a photo of Tristan and me walking into the bathroom. We were now a trending topic. I called my assistant and fired her.

I was ready for Chace to get home so I could talk to him about everything. I wondered if he had been informed. It was a small town. The world was my small town. I felt sick.

My anxiety was not unfounded. I had texted Chace after I left the library and still had no response. He always answered.

I polished off a bottle of wine before I got the nerve to text again. It was nine o'clock already and he had been off work for two hours.

Me: Where are you? I'm a little worried...
Chace: I'm staying with Andrew tonight.
Me: Oh. I wanted to tell you. Tristan flew here. He ambushed me at my book signing.
Chace: I heard.
Me: Oh. Are you mad at me?
Chace: No. But maybe we should cool this.
Me: Cool what?
Chace: Us. I don't think it's going to work.
Me: What? Why are you saying that?
Chace: It's okay. I know it was nothing serious.
Me: Yes. It was. It is. It could be. Whats going on?
Chace: I know you told Tristan that. I know that's how you feel about it. I just don't want the games. I said that from the beginning. I'm going to stay here for a while. I don't want it to

be weird. Can you please feed Artax tonight?

  Me: No, wait. Please just come here and I will explain. I just said that to get him out of here.

  Chace: I'm sorry. I don't feel like talking. Goodnight.

  Me: No, please, let's talk.

  Chace: I can't do this. You say you didn't mean it, that's fine. But with me, you mean what you say and you say what you mean. No drama. No mess. I don't want this. Goodnight. I'm turning my phone off.

I screamed into the silence of the field in front of me. Artax, lying next to me on the deck, jumped. I wiped at my eyes and threw my wine glass into the yard.

There was only one person I felt could have told Chace about the bathroom. His ex. I needed to find her. I was too tipsy to drive, so I called Kat to take me to the bar. It was a small town, maybe I would get lucky and find her.

As soon as Kat parked, I flew out of my seat and into the bar. Everyone turned when I walked in. They turned any time the door opened. It was habit.

There she was, perched on a barstool laughing. She turned her face to the door as I stepped in, just like the rest of them. I pointed towards the restroom. She rolled her eyes and slid off the stool.

She rounded the corner, entering the single stall room, I followed. Once again, I was having a confrontation in a bathroom. Awesome.

"What did you do?" I slammed the door behind us. I had no

doubt she had done something. It was in her eyes. A victory.

"I sent your little conversation to Chace." She shrugged, turning to the mirror to check her lip gloss.

"Please tell me you're lying." It was worse than I thought.

"No. Now he knows he is just a fling and you're using him to write. You can go home now. You're not needed. Chace and I are getting dinner tomorrow." Her reflection raised an eyebrow at me over her bare shoulder.

"That's a lie." I remember his words about her. He wasn't interested.

"No? Here. Look." She turned and shoved the glowing screen in my face. I read the tiny blue bubbles.

"He wanted you to delete the audio. Did you?"

"Yes." She pulled the phone away. Glaring.

"Simply because he asked." I laughed, condescendingly.

"Yes. I love him." I believed her. I did not need to question why. I almost felt sorry for her. He didn't love her.

"You really messed up." I shook my head.

"How's that?" She turned her chin up.

"You could have sold that audio to the tabloids and made money. You could have blackmailed me into giving you money. But no, you used it to try to get back with a man that doesn't even love you." I hoped the words stung. I needed her to hurt.

"Well he'll never love you now, either. So, I guess it was worth it." Her words hurt more.

"Are you okay?" Kat asked when we finally made it back to the parking lot. I had rushed past her from the bathroom. She quickly followed. I could feel the tears beginning to form. I hated crying. I rarely let it happen. I wasn't a pretty crier. But then, who was really? I willed them to go back into my body. They did not listen. Then they began to fall onto my shirt collar.

"No," I choked.

"What happened?"

"It's over." I knew it. I knew it in my gut. He had heard my voice. My voice saying words I did not mean. But they sounded real. It was over. I felt numb. I felt sick. I braced myself on the side of the car. I felt Kat's arm on my back. I turned into her embrace and let go.

I never cried when a relationship ended. They didn't warrant my sadness. They barely counted as relationships. I never cried when Tristan and I split. Well, I teared up a few times when the tabloids ripped into me, out of frustration, but never over the end of our relationship. I was sad, yes, but never sad enough to cry.

I felt as if something inside of me was gone. A hole was there. A piece I never knew lived within me, had flown away. A romantic. The one that died in me as a child. I felt Kat pulling away from me. She held me at arm's length and stared into my eyes. My face had to be a mess.

"I've never seen you like this. How serious was it between you two? Barely anything had happened right?"

She was right. We hadn't even had sex. Back home in New York, I wouldn't have counted this as anything, but here with him, it was different. I was myself with him. A self I didn't know existed.

The poet. The woman who wrote for herself, without fear and without worry. I was better because of him. Now, he was leaving me because he thought I was still the user I once was. The evidence was damning. I could not argue with it.

I stared into the sky above. Into the same stars we had been under on the deck. They taunted me. Magic didn't happen beneath them. My heart was breaking now under their gaze. The truth was a bitter pill to swallow.

"I love him," I said, broken.

I met Kat's eyes. She knew this sadness. I walked around her car to the passenger side. I got in and pulled my phone out. I loved him. So, I had to do the only right thing.

Me: I know your phone is off. I know you won't get this until morning. I just want to say how sorry I am. I didn't mean for this to happen. I break everything I touch. And you, you're the only one I will mourn. I know you don't believe me now. You don't trust me now. And that is my fault alone. I will be gone in a few days. You shouldn't have to leave your own home because of me. It is just as much yours as it ever was mine. I couldn't stay if I wanted. You're in every room. In every space. I will let you know when I am gone. Be happy. You gave me that gift. If only for a moment.

Twenty

May 14th

It seems I fell
in the spring.
That's me,
always tossing rules over my
shoulder,
dancing with
a siren's laugh in my throat,
warring with virginal ways
that do not do not do not suit
my inky flesh.

Summer is here & she
is lifting her skirt, begging
for a ride, playing
an unflinching game with
my grief-ridden eyes.

My haunting grounds cascade from
her whitewashed pockets

& she cackles with her sherbet lips.
Mulberry Project wine stained napkins
& promises to wipe
your phantom
amour away,
litter the hardwood.
Next to my resting place,
this bed you will never see.

My eyes narrow at
my white converse
by the door,
haphazard gravemarkers
smiling
at me.

Soles begging to
beat down to Albertine,
to become lost in words
that are strangers to you
& the way you
wounded me.

Twenty-One

June 20th

I've been here too long,
with shades drawn just as my eyes.
With the glow of a phone you never
send notes to, dimmed.

My knees keep my beating chest warm
& the mail is piled at the door.

I'm a runner.
It's what I do. You knew that.
You knew me.

The stars were afire the night
you pressed your ear to my breast
on that four post bed.

You listened for the chorus,
& the cadence,
& the cry.

There's a rhythm to goodbyes,
& I'm afraid you
were just waiting for one.

Soulmates aren't supposed to wound this way.
That's fairytale bullshit.
It's Disney dreams,
& I had others.

Before you
& the beat,
& the breath,
& the beauty you pulled out.

Now I believe
& it's not supposed to sound this way.
Like shattered glass & balloon drums.

I'm filled with a nameless taste,
some part of you
that won't go away.

I've been here too long,
with your goodbye
clutched tightly in my palms
that I hope the others
never have to know.

Twenty-Two

July 11th

I named you Ben today.
Last month you were Kyle.
The week before, Avery.
New names, every time.

I think I was writing about
you before we met.
I think I will write about
you long after
that lingering ache
from your lips
leaves me.

You fell for me before you touched my skin,
& I felt my essence in every note
you dropped onto the page.

I felt it in the songs you refused
to sing & the ones I caught

on that rainy balcony the
nights I held my breath &
inhaled the sound of your guitar.

I felt it in the way you lost
yourself in me, hidden
away on that mahogany bed
with the canopy & the rain.

I felt it when you
stopped taking my calls.
I felt it when I boarded my plane.
I felt it even when you
didn't stop me from running away.

Twenty-Three

August 30th

New York City is angry with me.
Her wails reverberate off the
volcano walls that
surround me.

We built a structure out of wickedness
& broken heels.
My sex, my sweat,
my sins were sweet.
She's a fiend, waiting
for old habits to itch my skin.

She smirks & ticks off temptations
on her tramp fingers.

"Terminal 5 & the man with the black hat?"
Yes, that was nice.

"Pianos & the cherry smoke he kissed into you?"

I think I can taste it, be quiet.

"Warsaw & the blue guitar?"
Oh, he was a fine lover.

She'll run out of digits,
listing nights I no longer
lean on.

Nights that fell
from my ribs
next to an Ozark tree line.
Where he grabbed my hand.
Where we raced the spring rain.

I dig his laughter from my
collarbone on days like this.
I place it on my tongue
& savor the taste
of lovers I ruin away.

Twenty-Four

September 29th

I'm thinking about running again.
Maybe to Alexandria.
I'll christen myself Kebechet,
I'll embrace my nature.

I'll tip toe down the
city sidewalks -
graceful.
I'll balance my halo,
I'll embrace my name.

I'll pretend among the
commuters
& work day warriors.
I'll forget I'm a vampire.

I'll fail to recall the flask
tucked
neatly into my coat pocket.

Let me pretend.
I tire of
being the villain.

Twenty-Five

October 23rd

The drapes don't move.
I've pulled them perfectly.
30 percent light let in.

I'm not drowning.
I'm not.

The clouds dance.
Puppet shows upon my thighs.
I will spend all day here.
Seated just so,
at an ebony dining table
overlooking the
stumbling
ants below
my window.

Sunday, every day is Sunday.
I had a dream that your voice

would grace my ears again as the
week yawned
& set itself to slumber.

Sunday, every day is Sunday.
I wait.
I cannot quit my wait.

November 13th

New York City in November is a magical thing. Twinkling Christmas lights begin to litter every storefront window. A crisp chill enters the air. I used to love it, back when I was carefree. When the demons I battled were bottled up and battled by men, liquor, and any other vice I could conjure up to keep them at bay. Now, I felt everything so clearly. I needed the pain.

Writing about heartbreak was not my specialty as an adult. I had succeeded in avoiding that pain and genre for so long. Now, I ached. I ached in places I didn't know existed. My body didn't want to function. And yet, the world was still turning. I couldn't fathom the fucking 'how' of it all. I simply wanted to stay in bed. Soulmates. I believed in that word now. This year I became a believer. What a bitch that was.

Seven months had passed since I left Missouri in a haze. After things ended with Chace, I went back to the old house we shared and tried to pack. Kat attempted to help. My hands didn't want to move. Eventually we ended up on the couch, watching movies until dawn. I did not sleep. My friend eventually passed out next to me, exhausted from the shared pain. She always absorbed.

I searched the phone book for a moving company as the sun crawled over the surface of my now hollow world. Hired movers would put my heartache in boxes. I visited my mother that day. I let her know I would be leaving. It broke her heart. She had seen a glimmer of hope that I would be staying for good. And I admit, I was starting to believe it too. Chace was not at her house. She had been asleep when he made it there the night before. Andrew was gone too. I was not able to tell him goodbye, either.

I had booked a hasty flight and said my goodbyes to Kat when she awoke that morning. I wanted out. I wanted to give Chace his normal life back. I wanted to give him his home back. I was the thorn and I needed to be removed. I didn't want to leave my friends and family. I wondered when I would see them again. I promised them it would be more often. I hoped my words were not as empty as my chest.

After making it back to New York, I went into hiding. I hardly left my apartment. I rarely saw the sun for the first few months. I slept and wrote. It was the only way I knew how to exorcise my pain. It barely worked. I hired a new assistant, since my last one sold me out. My new hire was given one golden rule to follow: to leave me out of everything.

I needed time to write out everything inside of me. I needed someone to keep the wolves at bay. My reclusiveness had a deadline. By late November I would need to be alive again. The final film would be releasing. I had until then to wallow in this misery.

My words were only for Chace. He was in every one of them. I sang for him, I bled for him, and the vein was heavy. Soon, I had enough, and I put my people to work on something new. Something real.

I announced my new project with a heavy heart and a queasy stomach. I didn't know how my fans would react or if they would even follow me on my new journey. I dipped my toe in slowly. I posted a few teasers from my poems on my Instagram,

Tumblr, and Facebook. I had my typewriter shipped back with the rest of my stuff. I tried not to read too many of the comments. They were always so hard to keep track of anyways. I had millions of followers.

I had bled too many words for a single poetry chapter book. So, I planned to release my work in three volumes. The first would release the Tuesday before the final film. Everyone on my team insisted it was the best move. I couldn't argue with that. I felt sick with it still. My heartbreak would be on display for the world, but so would my love. It was the only thing that kept me alive. For every poem I wrote about our end, my pain, and my loss, I wrote another about the time we had shared together. Though it was a small window of time, it was the most honest thing I had ever known.

I knew I had been a coward. Leaving the way I did. Just over 24 hours after breaking his heart, and my own, but that was the way I worked. I was a runner. Humans shed their skin every day, but some things are so deep inside, they can never be divorced from our skin.

Chace never texted me when he woke. I stared at my phone. I had checked it incessantly the day I packed my suitcase. Nothing. Just before I boarded my plane I texted him again. Letting him know he could come back home. Still, nothing.

Now, here I was, in November. My phone buzzing in my purse brought me back to the present. I paused in front of a glittering storefront and began fumbling in my bag. My gloved hands were clumsy. I wished I could say I was surprised by the name I saw on the screen. But I was not.

One person I did hear from often was Tristan. I rarely responded, and when I did, I was short with him. He was relentless. I still did not understand his fascination with me.

Okay, I did have some ideas. The fact that our movie premiere was quickly approaching was one. I shoved my phone back into my purse, pulled up my collar, and headed to my apartment.

It was just around the corner. I had an armful of presents, and they were making my limbs numb.

I would not be making it home for Thanksgiving. The guilt ate at me. I didn't want to pull away from my family again, but I was a coward. I couldn't face Chace just yet.

I was determined to conquer that fear by Christmas. Perhaps I was foolish. I knew a tiny part of me was hoping he would forgive me when my book came out.

Once inside my apartment, I unloaded my arms, and hung my purse. I didn't have much time. I was meeting Gemma for drinks. She wanted to celebrate my release week before all of the insanity began.

She was the only close friend I had in the City. She had taken care of me when I made it home, checking on me often, clearing my place of discarded food cartons. I had fired my housekeeper too. I wanted solitude.

We would be joined for drinks by her friend. Her male friend. Her gay male friend. There was something there. I felt that my friend was falling for him. I inquired about her feelings for him, but she quickly shot my suspicions down.

He was successful, smart, and beautiful. I could see how it would happen. The old me would have immediately went searching for a beautiful gay male to attempt to seduce, hoping for a story. Now, I just hoped my friend would be able to hold onto her heart.

I crept into my room and fell onto my bed. I grabbed my iPad from under my pillow. I had a few minutes before I needed to get dressed up. I saw the alert for Tristan's message again. Annoyed, I opened it.

Tristan: Can we please talk? I know I've been annoying as hell with these messages. But the premiere is next week. We need to be on the same page. How are we going to handle this?

"Handle this?" Handle what? The fact that the media dissected our every move still? You would think we were Brad Pitt and Jennifer Aniston. Would they ever get over our breakup? Okay, maybe it was nowhere near that level, but at times, it felt that way.

Me: We will smile for the cameras. We will pose in group pictures together. Hell, we will have pictures taken of the two of us together if they want that. You're an actor. I can fake it too. We will get through it.

Tristan: Will you be bringing a date?

Me: Why?

Tristan: If one of us brings a date and the other doesn't then that person is the asshole, and the other is the one everyone feels sorry for. It sucks all around. I know. I've dated costars where this kind of stuff came up. I'm sorry. But it is the truth. Maybe neither of us should bring someone.

Me: I did not plan on bringing anyone.

Tristan: Me either...

Tristan: Let's go together.

Me: No.

Tristan: I figured that would be your answer. I'll keep asking...

Me: Whatever you feel you need to do. Goodnight!

Tristan: Goodnight.

The man was unyielding. I had almost begun to feel bad for him. Months would go by with no reply from me and still, he texted at least once a week. Millions of women all over the world dreamed of being in my shoes. But he was not 'Tristan the movie star' to me. He was simply an ex who cheated. A blip on the map. He was not Chace.

It was because of him that I felt a certain softness towards Tristan. I was now in his shoes. I was not beyond yearning for an ex. I did not text Chace. I did, however, text my brother asking occasional questions. He humored me. Chace was not seeing anyone. Andrew told me he was back to working nonstop. Chace had wanted to take the summer off. My brother told me that did not happen. He enrolled in summer classes and worked often. I wondered if he needed the distraction. If I haunted him, too. I ached with the thought of him.

I pushed myself off my bed and stepped into my large closet. I pulled out a small black dress. A dress from the past. I couldn't remember the woman who used to wear it. I had thrown away every white dress I owned. I was not her anymore. Tonight would be the first time since coming home that I would be having alcohol with friends. Since moving home, I had given many things up. The only liquor consumed was the occasional glass of wine, at home. Sometimes I had two, while writing.

I had given up sex as well. I cleared out any numbers from my phone that had tempted me in the past.

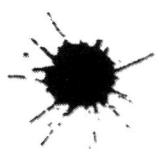

I met Gemma and her friend around the corner at one of my favorite bars. I found them in the back sitting in a small booth. They were seated close together, looking at something on his phone. The glow of his screen illuminated their faces.

I dropped my purse onto the table and scooted next to my friend. They both looked up, startled.

"You're heeeerrreee!" Gemma squealed. She turned in her seat to hug me. I noted the empty glasses on the table. I hugged her back.

"Am I late?"

"No, we got here early," she giggled. "I've had a few."

"Yes, I can see that." I caught the eye of a waitress and nodded. "I better catch up."

"I'm so glad you're here. I've missed getting drinks with you. I love you, Jaxt," she said as she turned to her guy friend and reached out, squeezing his arm, "but I need my best girl-friend." He chuckled in return.

"I know. I'm sorry," I said. "I've been a crappy friend this year. But the book is almost here. The writing is done. It's time for fun." I almost believed it. I was about 50/50.

After a few drinks, I found myself at 80/20. Some of my re-lease week nerves were slipping away. I was laughing. I hadn't laughed in so long. I think the last time was about a month ago at an episode of Friends when Ross went on and on about his sandwich. I had missed my friend. She and I did not have the history Kat and I shared, but she meant a lot to me.

Soon, we were giggling like fools. Jaxt did not drink much. He kept a watchful eye on Gem. I was glad for it. Despite my suspicions about her feelings for him, I was glad she had some-one to look out for her.

One in the morning rolled around quickly. Jaxt and Gemma walked me to my place and all the way up to my door. I hugged them both more than once. Before closing my door, I glanced back at them. They were holding hands and I felt an ache in my chest. I wanted that closeness again. That affection. I shouldn't have hid at home away from my friends all these months.

I stumbled to my bed and landed face first. I could feel re-gret forming slowly. I knew what I was going to do. It was an-other reason I had stayed away from alcohol. I grabbed my phone from the floor. The contents of my purse were dumped next to the bed. It wouldn't be too late where he was. I pulled up an empty message and typed.

Me: All of my words. They are for you.

I silenced my phone, tossed it across the room, crawled under my covers, and welcomed the black.

November 15th

I woke Tuesday with a multitude of emotions choking the air out of my bitter lungs. Fear, excitement, anxiety, numbness. In a few short hours, my first of three book signings scheduled for the week would kickoff. And, for the first time ever, I would be reciting a few poems.

It was so easy to hide behind the fiction of my writing. Too easy, I had been doing it for years. Hiding from the healing I desperately needed. This collection of poems was different. It was raw and real. It was a side of me the public had never seen. I didn't want to let my past grip me. I wanted to remove the anvil from my chest.

I had spent Monday nursing a hangover, and nursing the regret I felt over texting Chace. He never responded. The wound was open again. I wiped the tears that fell from my eyes the morning after, and refused to let any more fall. I could not think of it today. Ironically, it's all I would be thinking about today since I would be reading words inspired by him in front of so many people.

My mom texted me saying she wanted to be there for me

this week. I missed her. I needed her. I booked a flight for her right away. She would be by my side for all three signings, taking a cab straight over from the airport to the first bookstore.

I had sent her an advanced copy of my book. It made me nervous in a way I wasn't used to. I wrote explicitly sexual books. It never bothered me to know she may pick one up. This was different. This was not a character. This was me.

Nothing I hid from her about my childhood was in this volume of work. It would be in the second though. I could put off that panic attack, for a while.

Today was going to be fucking scary, but the day that second book came out would be... my stomach fell at the thought. I didn't want to think about it. It was next year. Another lifetime from now.

I shook my head and pulled myself away from the past, away from the future, and into the present. I got off my bed and walked to my closet. I pulled out my favorite dress. The one that made me feel luminous when I was scared. It was a leftover from the days of dating Tristan when I had a personal stylist. I didn't want to look ridiculous in front of the cameras that followed me around during our relationship. I didn't keep her long. It made me feel pretentious and silly.

As much as I hated to admit it, I did have a dress that would look better. Tristan had one sent over with a note that simply read "good luck this week." I groaned, but tried it on. It was perfect, it fit every curve. It hid the spots I was insecure about and highlighted the places I loved. Even still, I would not be wearing it. He didn't need a morsel to grab onto.

I wanted to text him and scold him about crossing lines, but with the premiere being this weekend I felt the need to keep the peace.

Book signings were insane. The energy I felt from my fans was tangible. I could feel it all around in the building. I could hear the murmur of their voices seeping through the walls that separated me from them.

I sipped once more from my bottle of water and concentrated on the music in my headphones. It was my ritual. Nothing but the sound of music for a half hour before the Q&A. Q&A's always took place before the signings.

I felt a hand on my shoulder. Gemma was letting me know it was time to go. I pulled my headphones off and downed the last of my water. I clenched my eyes and pressed my thumb into the spot between my eyebrows, trying to ease the ache there.

"Are you ready?" Gemma asked.

I looked up into her warm eyes. She squeezed her hand just a bit and I smiled. I was glad I had asked her to help out today. I needed the support.

"Yes," I lied. I wasn't but I didn't have a choice. I smoothed down the fabric on my thighs and stood. I walked to the edge of the stage, hidden by the curtain. She walked out ahead of me.

I concentrated on the floor as I heard her talking to the crowd. The low rumble of their laughter in response to her voice met my ears. I didn't know what she was saying. I was lost staring at my designer shoes. They looked foreign on my feet. I had been walking around my apartment for months, barefoot. When I left, the rare times I did, I wore the white converse I had often thrown on in Missouri. I stared at the toecap often, wondering what date to write on them, but that was Chace's thing, and I wouldn't do it.

I was pulled away from my red-soled high heels by the

sound of applause. Gemma came back behind the curtain and put her hands on my shoulders, staring at me full on.

"You can do this," she urged. I set my jaw and reached up for her wrists, nodding. She stepped aside and I walked out onto the stage.

The sound was overwhelming. I had heard it before. I had felt it before, but this was different. I was proud of my work. I was proud of myself. Inexplicably, a smile spread onto my face. It wasn't forced, it wasn't strained. It felt strange and beautiful. I took a seat on a stool with a microphone next to it.

Gemma reached in front of me and grabbed the microphone, starting the madness.

"To start things off we will have the Q&A," she directed. "Raise your hands when the time comes and I will pick who gets to ask a question."

She handed the microphone to me and stepped back. I reluctantly grabbed it and cleared my throat.

"First I just want to thank you all for coming," I started. "The support I have received over the years has been, unbelievable. I do not know what I have done to deserve you all. This has been a scary journey. I am not the woman I was before. I am always growing, changing, moving. We all are, right?" The crowd chirped in agreement. "You make me proud to have taken this step." Chace had helped me get here. I paused, and then pushed my chair back.

"I know this is different. This is not what is expected from me. But I could not be more proud than I am right now. As a poet, you leave it all out there. If anyone has ever wondered who I am, who the author behind the page is, the answer is in your hands right now."

I wondered how many had read it cover to cover already. The bookstore had already been open for eight hours. I wanted to know what they thought. I looked back at Gemma letting her know I was ready. She nodded. I turned back to see hands in the air.

"Okay yes, you." I heard my friend's voice from behind me. I began walking around the stage, pacing. A young girl in what looked to be her early twenties began speaking.

"When did you write your first poem?" He eyes smiled at me. I felt a warmth work through me.

I thought back. It felt so long ago. "I was, honestly, I don't remember. Maybe nine?" Writing about pain no child should know but that too many knew. They needed to know they weren't alone.

More hands shot up. Another fan was chosen, a woman about ten years or so older than me. "Will you be writing another trilogy series?"

I was prepared for this question. It was asked online constantly. I wanted to be honest. No bullshit. "At this point I don't know. I'm just going to let my writing guide me. I'm going to go where my heart leads me. If I feel a new story, then yes. Right now I am going to focus on my poetry and this collection."

More hands. "What made you decide to focus on poetry?"

It was a simple answer. A one word answer. Chace. "Well," I paused. "Someone. I met someone this year who gave a new meaning to my life. Someone who gave me a newfound confidence in myself."

I saw movement next to the stage and looked over. My mother was here. She had my book clutched to her chest and her suitcase parked next to her. She gave me a reassuring smile. I took a deep breath and tuned back to the crowd at the sound of Gemma's voice choosing another person.

"Is it the person you dedicated the book to? Chace?" It was out there for the world. His name.

"Yes," I nodded.

More hands. "Are all the poems about him?"

I looked over at my mother briefly. "No. Not all of them. I touched on many kinds of love in this collection. The love I have for my family is in there. For my friends. And the love I have for you all. Those are all in there as well. I learned a lot about that four-letter word this year. I've always known the love of family, friends, and my fans, but I had never been in love. That changed this year."

I knew I shouldn't have said it. I knew I shouldn't have dismissed my relationship with Tristan so close to the movie premiere, but I was tired of faking it for the camera, faking it for the world. It was the truth, and I needed to stop hiding. Chace was the first man I had ever loved. I wanted him to be the last.

The questions lasted just under a half an hour. They were much of the same. Tristan's name was not brought up, much to my relief. I suppose no one wanted to be the one to bring it up. Instead, I was asked what I would be wearing to the movie premiere this Friday. I was always happy to talk fashion. I would take that over drama any day.

We took a short bathroom break between the questions and the reading. I was able to talk with my mother. To hug her. It had been so long since she had been to a signing.

When I made my way back to my seat on the stage, nerves set in again. I clutched my book in my hands. Gemma informed the crowd I would be reading only ten poems, reader-chosen, so that we could get to the signing portion of the event.

I hoped they would take it easy on me. I hoped they wouldn't pick only the words that said his name over and over.

"**P**age 68," the girl said. I knew what poem that was. I didn't need to turn to it, but I did anyway, for show. I felt a little frozen. I felt myself go back to the day I wrote it. Not long after I flew home.

I had been home a little less than a week. My phone stayed off for days. So many people were pissed at me. My mother. Kat. Gemma. My brother. They wanted to kill me. I just needed the silence. I needed to be alone.

I hated myself. My reasons had been endless. I hated myself for running way, again. I hated myself for not fighting for Chace. I hated myself for falling in love with him.

I did not need the pages. I looked up from my book, into the crowd, and my eyes caught on blue. They caught on someone who was not there before. How the fuck was this happening? Chace was standing at the back of the crowd.

All I could see was azure. His eyes were all I knew. I needed to start speaking. I needed to recite this poem, but he was in the room with me. And all the air had left with his entrance.

The side of his mouth turned up. It was the most beautiful sight I had ever seen. I returned his smile and my eyes welled. I smiled like a goddamn idiot. I knew it. I knew I looked like a fool. I surveyed the crowd. Some of them were looking back at Chace. I looked up into the light above me for a moment, willing the tears away. I looked back down into his eyes, cleared my throat and began speaking.

The room remained silent as each poem fell from my lips. I tried not to fumble over the words in his presence. After I had read the last one I heard the murmur of voices in the crowd, they broke my concentration on the piece I had just recited. I looked over at Gemma and my mother. Their eyes were wide. They were trained on something behind me. I turned around, and felt my heart sink.

Tristan made his way up the steps to me, smiling and waving to the guests. The crowd erupted. The noise was deafening. He reached for the microphone in front of me, pulling it from its cradle.

"Hello everyone," he greeted. "I'm sorry to show up like this. I won't take long. I know you're all eager to get your books signed by this beautiful woman right here. I just wanted to stop by and tell her how proud I am of her. If you haven't read this wonderful collection of words yet, just know, you are going to be blown away. I have never in my life met a talent like her. I am so happy to have her in my life."

I felt sick. I couldn't move. I looked back at Chace. He was gone. No. Please, no. Not again. FUCK!!! I jumped from my seat and made my way to the side of the stage. Gemma and my mother caught me.

"You can't go. You still have to sign," Gemma pleaded.

I could hear Tristan talking to the crowd. "He did it again. He keeps fucking everything up. I have to find Chace," I said through clenched teeth, pushing past her.

My mother caught me. "Hun, you can't leave. You have a commitment here. We will figure it out. I'll call him," she said, squeezing my arms.

"Please. Please tell him I did not ask that idiot to come here. Oh my fucking hell, Mom. Did you know Chace was going to be here?" My voice had reached an inhuman pitch.

"Yes. I'm so sorry. He flew with me. He wanted it to be a surprise. We are going to fix this." She had her reassuring mom voice on. I reached for her hand.

"Please. Please call him. I can't do this again. I can't lose him before I even get him back."

"I'll call him. You just stay here. Sign those books. This is your moment. I am so proud of you."

She pressed a kiss to my forehead, grabbed her suitcase, and walked away. I stayed frozen to the stage and watched her go. I was terrified.

November 15th

The signing was a blur. I was a zombie. I was ashamed of myself by the end of it all. I was not who they came to see. My sorrow was painted on my face. My rage towards Tristan was there too. I tried my best to smile at the cameras and chat though. My mind was gone. It was off chasing Chace.

After, I found a message from my mother on my phone; she was unable to reach him. All hope was lost. He probably changed his flight, flew away from the mess of us. Just like I had done months ago. I couldn't even blame him. It was a scene straight out of a typical romantic comedy. Except I wouldn't be getting my cookie cutter bullshit happy ending.

I called my doorman to let my mother in and informed her I would meet her back there in a couple hours. I walked the streets. I had a limited amount of time with her, but I needed to be alone. I did not want to put myself through the readings the next two days. I thought I could separate myself from the heartache in those pages, but now it was wide open once more. The wound was fresh. A crimson ribbon floating in the November breeze behind me.

I was done with Tristan. I would no longer spare him. I

would no longer try to be civil. We would never be friends. I found him lingering around the bookstore after the signing and I let him know. I think, in his eyes, I finally saw his resignation.

I wandered the streets. I wandered my mind. The madness would be back again. The melancholy. My music was gone. Again. Fucking. Again. Life was black and white cylinder solitude.

Eventually I found myself back on my street. I wasn't aiming that way intentionally, but here I was. I needed to get home anyway. My mother was surely worried.

My leaden feet carried me up the steps. I opened my door to darkness. The soft light of my nightlight in the kitchen glowed. Why was my mom hanging out in the dark?

"Mom? Where are you?" I rounded the corner, into my kitchen. It was not my mother standing there. I choked on my breath. I pressed my palm to my chest.

"I'm sorry. I shouldn't be here. Your mom let me in," Chace said in one breath. His palms in the air, greeting me.

"It's okay, really." I didn't know if I had actually said it out loud. I must have because he nodded.

"No, it isn't. Look, I know we broke up a long time ago. Honestly, I don't even know if we were a couple. And if you're with Tristan now, I understand." He shook his head, bit his lip, and continued. "I let you go. I didn't try to stop you. I regretted it. I came home the day after you flew here and I hated that house. I hated not having you in it. I called you. I called so many times. Your phone went straight to voicemail. I tried for days and I couldn't get through. I should have believed you then. I did believe you. Still, I let you go. I was just so damn scared. I probably pushed you right back into his arms. But when you texted me the other day, I couldn't breathe. I figured your mom had an advanced copy of your book so I asked her for it. I read the dedication. And I knew."

I read the words in my head. The ones I hoped he would

find. The key to finding the ones I had hidden, back beneath the floorboard.

'For Chace.
I hope one day, again, you'll find me.
You're the only one who knew where to find me.'

"I went back to that spot. I found the poems you wrote while you were in Missouri. Then I read what was published. Was it true? Was everything you wrote true?" His whispery voice fluttered to me. I was always flustered and fumbling around him.

"Yes. Yes yes yes." I took a step towards him.

"You were in love with me?"

"I am." I didn't know a before.

"You are now?"

"Yes. I am not with Tristan. That performance was just another of his stunts. I am so fucking in love with you."

It was out of my mouth before I could stop it. He stared back into my eyes. I saw his hand clench the countertop. I wanted him to cross the space in between. I wanted him to reach for me, but we just stood there, like two people who had never touched, both scared to make the first move.

It needed to be me. I had spoken the words, but words were nothing, if not followed up by actions. I had fantasized about having him here in front of me every day since I left Missouri. I wrote him back to me over and over. I wrote it so many ways, but none were like this. Reality has a way of being so much more beautiful than the pictures words paint.

I walked slowly around the island, to where he stood, leaning against my counter. He was still, his jaw locked, his hands tense on the granite behind him.

He did not move. He just watched. Maybe he was scared. Maybe he wasn't ready even though he flew thousands of miles.

I reached my hand out, and lightly set it on his own. He turned it over and grabbed on, pulling my hand behind my back. He stood over me, using his other hand to tip my chin back. I looked into his eyes.

"I don't know what it feels like to not be in love with you," he whispered. His lips were on me all at once. My hands fisted in his shirt. He backed me up into the island, his hands making their way to my hair. It was as if we never parted. The hole inside of me was instantly filled.

I started grinning wildly, halting our kiss. Chace pulled away, smiling back.

"I know," he said. He didn't need to say anything else. We kissed again, frantically. There wasn't anything more to say. Not now.

Our hands and lips were magnets, I didn't know where he ended and I began. He walked me backwards around the island. I felt my ass bump into a barstool.

Chace reached for my hips and lifted me up onto it. I wrapped my legs around his waist, pulling him in. He pulled his mouth away from mine and I moved forward instinctively. I opened my eyes to his. To the blue, I had missed.

I had been living my life in blue hues without him. I felt music inside my heart again. He was my music. I couldn't live without it again. I was merely madness and melancholy without him.

"Tell me again," he whispered, leaning his forehead against mine.

"I am so fucking in love with you, Chace."

He kissed me again, long and slow, his hands deftly finding their way to the zipper of my dress. I felt the cool metal move down my spine as it made its descent.

One of the most beautiful things about Chace had always been his calm. The calm that balanced out my manic mind. He was steady, and I simply flowed around him, in waves, in drops, in floods. I felt him coming undone. He had spent his whole life gluing himself back into a whole man and I felt him coming apart under my hands.

He didn't feel scared. I always wanted control, but he had it now, even as he came undone. He had me. I felt his power. I felt his strength. He was the strongest person I had ever met.

His mouth made its way to my neck. I leaned back, inviting him in, digging my heels into his ass. I thanked myself for choosing such a billowy dress, one that did not bind my legs.

Chace's hands made their way to the straps of my dress, pulling them over my shoulders. My breath picked up, the rise and fall of my breasts, caught his eye. My nude cotton push up bra cupped me. He exhaled, my fingers clenched on the skin beneath his shirt.

He reached his arms over his shoulders and quickly pulled his shirt off over his head. His eyes fell onto my chest again, and then his mouth landed there, he reached a hand up and pulled the right cup down. My heartbeat quickened.

He reached down, pulling the bar stool closer, away from the island. With his other hand he grabbed my wrist, and pulled it behind my back, he did the same with my other hand, securing them with one of his own, behind me.

He took his finger and brushed the hair from my neck. The long strands slipped over me, hardening my peak.

When his mouth found its way down I nearly bucked off the stool. Chace groaned and lightly nibbled, sending me further into ecstasy. He traced the tip, teasing, testing.

This was different from any first time I had ever had. The night we almost went the distance, he had been so shy, so timid. I pulled his hips closer, heat was rising. I needed a release, and we had barely started.

He had a way of doing this to me. Intimacy was foreign, and I felt it, here. There was a charge in his touch, in his breath, and my pulse tried to keep up.

I was a virgin to making love. To me, it was always just a cheesy expression. It wasn't real. It was for romantics and silly lovers. This, was beautiful. This, I knew, would define us.

He released the grip on my wrists, both hands landed on my thighs, pushing my dress up higher, his mouth never left my breast.

I grabbed the bar behind me, laying my head back, trusting him to hold me up. His mouth left me and I straightened, looking for him. He leaned down, his fingers finding the warm fabric between my legs. He pushed it to the side and slid his finger over the center of me. Then he was parting me, it was simple. I was ready.

I had been ready the moment he touched me. His mouth was close, I could feel his breath. I was nervous. I had had many men down there, but he had me on edge. He was the only one who mattered. I wasn't going to put on a show, dramatics, theatrics.

When his tongue found my warmth, I nearly died, silently. I clenched my eyes and felt a tear roll down my cheek. I felt clean. I felt new. He worked me to the brink then came up to rest his lips upon my neck, pulling my panties down quickly. I opened my eyes and saw his own taking in the salt staining my cheeks.

"Are you okay?" he asked, moving his hands to my face, his eyes searching.

"Yes," I whispered. I lied. It's what I do. I crossed my arms over my chest. A reflex. I covered my heart and my traitor lungs.

"You're safe with me," he assured, simply.

I nodded in response, murdering my bottom lip, trying to avoid his gaze. I desired the ability to be open, but a fear was still living inside of me, maybe I would never be free of it. I wanted to; I couldn't live in this skin prison forever.

"Look at me, please." I clenched my eyes and shook my head. He tried again. "Seraphina."

My eyes flew open and I turned to him, locking into him. He held me there. "You're not a dirty thing," he told me.

"You're not the things you wrote in your poetry as a child. You're not damaged. You're not a scar. Your grandfather was a bad man. You are nothing but good. He did not ruin you. No fucking way. I know what he did to you. I know why you had their room taken out during the remodel. I know you beat yourself up over the fact that you didn't go to his funeral, that your mother thinks you had pneumonia and you punish yourself for that lie. I know you can't look at tulips, his favorite flower. Your mother wanted them planted around the house. I told her I couldn't find any. When she did and planted them, I yanked them out of the flowerbed before you moved back. I told her that rabbits got to them."

I choked out a sob at his words and rested my forehand on his shoulder. He reached up and rested his palm on my cheek, then leaned down and spoke into my hair.

"You hold this darkness deep inside your ribcage. I know how that feels. I have it too. It isn't the same as yours, I know that, but your darkness is fucking blinding, Sera. It's beautiful and it's a part of you. Use it."

"How?" I whimpered.

"Let it out. Write about it again. Show it to everyone. Show it to no one. But please, don't let it sit in there anymore." He took his hand from my face and placed it over my heart. I leaned back and looked into his endless blue. "It's a cancer and I need you with me."

I uncovered myself and wrapped my arms around his neck. I pulled him in, to my skin and my broken bits. I wept and he stayed steady.

I recalled a poem I wrote when I returned home from Missouri, once I escaped that house again and the slow choke of my memories.

some people are
born fractured.

demons deposited
here among us.

I like to think I was born pure.
that for a while I was like an angel.
(my mother named me after one, after all)

I guess it wasn't in the master plan for me to
stay that way.
this sickness was put inside of me
by familiar hands.

I walk with the pretty people now.
the good.
but I am not.

I am not good.

Chace made love to me that night. It was tender and rushed and then a slow resurrection. He was vulnerable and I was a soft cry in the low light of my bedside lamp. He bit my jaw and followed the map of my pulse. He tasted my tears and the pure passion I wrote about but never allowed myself to give into. I let him take control, something I never did. He let me unravel.

He reminded me that I am good.

Chace

Sera told her mother about the childhood abuse she experienced at the hands of her grandfather while we were all still in New York. They sat on her bed all day and wept together. I brought them food and water and stayed away, letting them have the moment, the one she had been hiding from her for years.

The guilt Sera had been choking on was unnecessary. Now, she was free. They were the two strongest women I had ever met. They would heal together. They would not let that man ruin, again, not even from the grave.

I stayed in the City for the rest of Sera's signings, and then we flew back to Missouri together. We stayed in Sera's mother's house, while she figured out what she wanted to do with her grandparent's old home, her old home, my old home. I knew what she would decide, but I stayed quiet and waited for her to work through it in her own way.

I held her on the nights she would cry silently into her own pillow. I brushed the hair away from the back of her neck and kissed her there, whispered there. I listed all the ways she had changed me. All the reasons I would never leave her side. She had been holding everything deep in her chest for so long, letting it eat away at her light, letting it cloud the mirrors she looked into. Each day I saw a bit of her self-loathing fall away.

We spent two months moving everything out of the old farm-house. The books, the beds, the vanity, and the china her mother loved. She had some moved into storage, sold some, and burned some in the front yard. I would sit on the front porch and watch as she doused pieces in gasoline. I would watch as she let it go. She would wait a moment, watching the flames going higher, and then she would come back to me. She would take a seat and grip my hand. She watched the black smoke fill the sky, and I watched her breathe deep and exhale.

When it was all done, she had the house demolished. She kept the land, not wanting to sell the woods that were her refuge all those years. We sat in the treehouse, out in the green, away from prying eyes, as the bulldozers ripped it all apart. She sat at the old school desk, her knees pressed together, her head in her hands, dark hair tumbling towards the floor. I sat on that old futon for a while, watching her.

After a moment, I walked over to her and knelt down to her feet. She was wearing her white converse. I pulled a sharpie from my pocket and reached for her ankle. She jumped, pulled from her thoughts, and looked at me. "What are you doing?" She asked.

"You can let it go today," I said. I pulled the cap off with my teeth and looked down at her feet, then back up at her. "Today is the start of something new. A blank canvas."

She nodded and a tear started to roll down her cheek. I wrote the date on her shoe quickly then threw the marker over my shoulder, reaching for her.

I was born to touch Sera. Whether she was falling apart or putting me back together, it did not matter. I had fallen in love with her when I was a young boy. Before I had a chance to go out and see the world. I had no regrets. Falling for someone so young was not a burden, as my mother had thought. I could barely remember a time before her, her words, and the comfort she planted in me. A day didn't pass by without me reminding her of how she saved me, how we had saved each other.

After I finished school, Sera and I moved to Nashville. I found a teaching job there and wrote music in the moments I had to spare. Together, we designed a writing workshop for the troubled youth in the area. Lyrics, poetry, and short stories. We recruited singers and songwriters in the Music City to help.

We made our home downtown, in a one-bedroom loft apartment above our classroom. We thought about finding a house outside of Nashville eventually, but the hours we spent downstairs were long, and rewarding. We couldn't imagine cutting them short, even for a commute.

Sera became a voice for the abused. Her second book of poetry set her secrets free for the world to see. As emails and messages came in from strangers all over the world, telling her that her courage had changed them, I watched her change.

Others knowing they were not alone helped them to let their own voices be heard. She helped them believe they could one day break free.

Working with those children, helped me let go of the resentment I had held onto towards my father. I couldn't let it eat at me anymore. I reached out to him; I reached through the casual conversation we had been drowning in for years and he reached back. I didn't wear my darkness like a shroud, the way Sera had, but it was still there, deep down. Each time I spoke to my father, I felt some of it fall away.

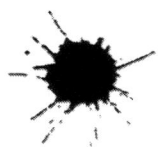

After three years together, I asked Sera to marry me, as we relaxed in her old four post bed, listening to the rain pelting our downtown Nashville home. Our floor-to-ceiling windows let the yellow glow of street lamps in, painting her skin gold. She closed her amber eyes and reached for the only thing she was wearing, a hand stamped necklace circling her neck, the one she never took off.

I laughed when she had it made. I smiled. She infused beauty into my skin. She called me her music. She wrote poetry about it. 'He is music, and I am merely madness and melancholy'. She wore those words around her neck, her love for me. She was not merely madness and melancholy. She was so much more. I was convincing her, every day.

She rubbed her thumb back and forth over the words and then opened her eyes. "Yes," she breathed.

I reached for her, pulling her close. She wrapped her legs around my center and found my lips. I poured my dreams into her collarbone and she kept them there, safe. I rocked into her and felt everything fall away. She let me love her without restraint. She let me unravel.

She reminded me that I am good.

Acknowledgments

Writing this book is one of the hardest things I have ever done. Without these people, it never would have happened.

Krystal and Courtney, my book club besties. Never change. I love when you are hangry and when you over do it and when you think you may die. I love meeting once a month to be assholes and all the texting in between.

My Radiant Sky family. I am so glad I have found a home with you beautiful humans. We are going to change the world.

Kat, it was fate we met. I wrote you into this book before we ever met! How spooky is that? You're my go-to. My confidant. Your words heal and I can't wait to see all that you do this year.

Alicia, my editor and friend. Thank you for never trying to change my voice. You polish my mess and make it lovely, while still keeping my jagged edges. I'm sorry I hate capitalization and punctuation. I'm sorry I may never change.

Beta readers, bloggers, critique partners, and research gatherers. Talon, Katoff, Christina, Stephanie, Devon, and the rest of you brave souls. Thank you for reading this through all of the phases.

TJ, thank you for the valuable NYC information.

Mom, thank you for showing me what true strength is and for showing me unconditional love. You showed me that we can live full lives, despite our past.

Aaron, thank you for believing my truth, and for never doubting me.

Brandon, thank you for showing me what true goodness looks like in this world.

Catye, thank you for showing me friendship—unflinching. For telling me your secrets. For guarding my own. For having my back, through every up and down. We will have so many stories to tell when we are sitting side by side in our rockers with white hair and too many wrinkles around our eyes. I'll have more, of course, because gingers never age.

Cody, where do I begin? We have had a long crazy ride, full of messes and forgiveness. You balance me. I would be tumbling around this world, lost, without you. You saved me. It was as simple as that, but it was never simple.

J.R. Rogue is very active on social media and encourages you to follow her around.

Instagram
https://www.instagram.com/j.r.rogue/

Facebook
https://www.facebook.com/jrrogueauthor/

Facebook user group
https://www.facebook.com/groups/1627799237440695/

Twitter
https://twitter.com/jenR501

Website
www.jrrogue.com

Made in the USA
Charleston, SC
23 June 2016